Francis Saltus Saltus

Shadows and Ideals

Francis Saltus Saltus

Shadows and Ideals

ISBN/EAN: 9783337042271

Printed in Europe, USA, Canada, Australia, Japan

Cover: Foto ©Andreas Hilbeck / pixelio.de

More available books at **www.hansebooks.com**

SHADOWS AND IDEALS

POEMS

BY

FRANCIS S. SALTUS.

L'ART *a des frontières, la* PENSÉE *n'en a pas.*

—VICTOR HUGO.

BUFFALO
CHARLES WELLS MOULTON
1890

CONTENTS.

CONTENTS.

xiii

THE CLOUD.

I.

When light first dawned upon the startled Earth,
In storm and wild confusion I had birth ;
Tossed by impetuous winds on every side,
   I traversed countless leagues of fiery air
   Filled with dull thunder or the lightning's glare,
Wondering at God's omnipotence and pride.

II.

From chaos and from nothingness I came,
Borne on the wings of a creative flame ;
While far below me I could hear the roar
   And exultation of the new-born seas,
   Moaning their joy of life unto the breeze,
Beating with jubilant waves upon the shore.

III.

God willed that I for centuries should roam,
With rest denied, upon their breasts of foam,
Gazing upon a sad unpeopled strand,
    Until the glory of His might appeared,
    And rugged trees with swaying boughs upreared
Their leafy loveliness at His command.

IV.

Sweet birds were born and flew for shelter there;
Blithe carolings of rapture filled the air;
And, lo ! upon the grassy slopes below
    I saw strange monsters in the rivers wade,
    And hideous serpents writhing in the shade,
Or basking in the sunlight's freshest glow.

V.

Drifting from mountains of eternal ice
To balmy islands redolent with spice,
I marked the silent progress of His power.
    And from my bosom on the pregnant plain
    Issued the fecund ripple of my rain,
While the young Earth became one blooming bower.

VI.

I could not know the fate God held for me,
And, passive, wandered over land and sea,
Now black with storms, now lurid with swift fire ;
   And when the tempests ceased and were no more,
   To starry heights in silence I would soar,
A slave of God, unconscious of desire.

VII.

Of gold auroras I would form a part,
Or linger, swooning, in the torrid heart
Of angry Hecla thundering forth its praise
   In fiery showers ascending to God's throne ;
   And then again for countless years alone,
I passed in calm the uneventful days.

VIII.

The glorious bow of Heaven in luminous light
Lent me its various hues, and in the night
The gentle stars guided my path thro' space,
   And I enjoyed the inestimable boon
   Of floating o'er the white brow of the moon,
And gazing on the marvel of its face.

IX.

Strange changes came, but brought me no release ;
My aimless journey was not doomed to cease,
And ages passed before I saw the Earth
  By God into an Eden of beauty wrought;
   While Man, created like myself from naught,
Had in this awful lapse of time found birth.

X.

His seed had flourished, and on every side
I, marveling, saw the traces of his pride,
Cities and temples, monuments and towers !
  Music was born, while mirth usurped dull fear,
   And from my azure birthplace I could hear
Melodious reeds that charmed the weary hours.

XI.

No longer was I hurried by the storms,
But over Babel I could count the forms
Of rebel mortals who had dared aspire
  To scale high Heaven, and I saw their woe
   When God no more withheld the avenging blow,
But filled their fields and cities with His fire.

XII.

And, lo ! base Sodom, in its odious shame,
I saw destroyed in vivid sheets of flame,
That volleyed thro' me rushing thro' the skies ;
  And after, by a sceptered king's command,
  I saw grave nations toiling in the sand,
From which gigantic Cheops was to rise.

XIII.

Wafted by shifting winds from shore to shore,
I gazed upon the splendors of Lahore,
Its golden domes and avenues of palms,
  Where dusky bayaderes, with jeweled hands,
  Danced by the moon lascivious sarabands,
Reeking with unguents and delicious balms.

XIV.

Where Nankin's porcelain turrets pierce the sky,
Free from alarming storm, I wandered by
And saw the haughty dragoned flags unfurled
  O'er golden kiosks, where Mongol warriors pass,
  And where the Hoang-ho, thro' the flowery grass,
Like some huge, silver serpent, idly curled.

XV.

Bel-Shar-Uzzur upon his ivory throne
In mighty Babylon I saw alone ;
And in the spicy temples of great Bel
 I saw each virgin that was once Ishtar's,
 With eager lips and eyes that beamed like stars,
Pray that Mylitta would her bliss foretell.

XVI.

Karnac and Memphis, Nineveh and Tyre
Taught me their life, their tumult, their desire ;
And o'er the sparkling seas of misty foam
 I saw great Cæsar in his chariot stand,
 A glaive victorious in his valiant hand,
Hailed by the exultant clamorings of Rome !

XVII.

Then came a day of wonderment and pain
To me, poor wanderer over hill and plain,
To me, who trembled at the odious sight ;
 For subtle powers urged me from lea to lea,
 Until, beneath me, I again could see
Jerusalem all glittering in light.

XVIII.

And, lo ! great crowds of frenzied people crushed
The paths of Pilate's palace as they rushed,
Driving before them with atrocious cries
   A pale, meek, suffering man, who made no sign,
   But stood in sorrow, beautiful, divine,
With thorn-crowned brows and pardon in His eyes.

XIX.

They dragged Him forth to Calvary and death;
I heard the hurried flutter of His breath,
And saw Him bend beneath the cross He bare.
   Helpless I heard the crushing of each nail,
   Piercing His palms, and saw His brow turn pale,
But no appeal for mercy rent the air.

XX.

The bearded soldiers pricked Him with their spears,
The rabble laughed and shouted at His tears,
While gall was tendered to His blistered lips,
   Till, suddenly, he prayed — and then the skies
   Were rent asunder, and His suppliant eyes
Gazed on the heavens' wrath in strange eclipse.

XXI.

The florid day changed to a sudden night,
While people fled in tumult and affright,
And dizzy lightnings warned them of their doom ;
　　But He was left upon the cross to die,
　　Without a guardian, prayer, or pitying eye,
To cheer the odious pathway to the tomb.

XXII.

And, lo ! He perished in His nameless pain,
While from my breast there fell consoling rain,
Too late, alas ! His sufferings to allay ;
　　And in the midnight those who loved Him came,
　　His tortured body as their own to claim,
And with hot tears they carried it away.

*　　*　　*　　*　　*

XXIII.

Then I remained in wonder and surprise,
Deprived of motion in the sultry skies,
Until three dawns had passed ; then subtler change
　　Passed through me as I lingered calmly still,
　　Mute and obedient to a higher will,
Filled with presentiments divine and strange.

XXIV.

A something sweet, and mystic, and divine,
A feeling all mysterious was mine :
I felt a buoyant gladness uncontrolled,
  While, lo ! a dazzling change came over me,
  And people on the plains below could see,
With marveling eyes, that I had turned to gold.

XXV.

Radiant, resplendent, I hung breathless there,
When, lo ! approaching through the silent air,
A resurrected shape forsook the sod,
  And, ere I knew my happiness unpriced,
  I felt the pure and spotless form of Christ,
Pass through me on the way to meet His God.

June, 1884.

ROME'S MAGNIFICENCE.

Oft through the mazes of the Roman mart
    And quaint Trastevere I have strolled alone ;
    And, in St. Peter's miracle of stone,
Have felt the awe of God pervade my heart.

The stately city in its every part
    Has to mine eyes its greatest splendor shown.
    Its loves, and pains, and sufferings I have known,
Its dizzy Carnival, its peerless Art !

The Vatican recalls delicious days,
    And, with the flawless, mellow moon o'erhead,
        Through august ruins I have wandered free.
But, oh ! I marvel at all, yet dare not praise ;
    On yonder green Campagna *she* lies dead,
        And what is Rome's magnificence to me ?

THE BAYADERE.

Near strange, weird temples, where the Ganges' tide
  Bathes domed Lahore, I watched, by spice-trees fanned,
  Her agile form in some quaint saraband,
A marvel of passionate chastity and pride.

Nude to the loins, superb and leopard-eyed,
  With fragrant roses in her jeweled hand,
  Before some Kaât-drunk Rajah, mute and grand,
Her flexile body bends, her white feet glide.

The dull Kinoors throb one monotonous tune,
  And wail with zeal as in a hasheesh trance;
    Her scintillant eyes in vague, ecstatic charm
Burn like black stars below the Orient moon,
  While the suave, dreamy languor of the dance
    Lulls the grim, drowsy cobra on her arm.

SELFISHNESS.

The sky was weird with storm and coming night,
   While, mute with hate, I paced the dismal street.
The restless adders of my passion's spite
   Hissed in my heart, and yet I found them sweet.

Oblivious to all, I did not hear
   Reverberant thunders swoon upon the air!
And knew not that my path was darkly drear,
   I, with no Mecca, wandering anywhere!

But sudden the dusk of Heaven before my eyes
   Broke, and, with scintillant throbs of livid blue,
A snake of lightning writhed along the skies,
   Rending the voids of cloud it shuddered through!

Though dazed and blind, I shrieked unto the night:
   " Strike me, blue grandeur, ere again we part!
Scorch me to dust, thou awful god of light,
   Burn unto hell the hate that is my heart! "

Again the flash of quivering sheen shot by,
   Charring all near me, and I cried out still:
" Coward ! why spare ? Oh, if I can not die,
   Give me at least thy peerless power to kill ! "

But all in vain, oh ! insolence sublime !
   What power would pause *my* wrongs to vindicate,
Which, while I *thought*, could, for the millionth time,
   Encompass earth with its own lurid hate !

REPASTS.

I.

Within a garret where all fire is dead,
A poet dreams of Fame and seeks his bed,
Avidly gnawing a foul crust of bread.

II.

A fair young mother, happy and elate,
Fills with kind hand her little darling's plate,
The first real Christmas meal he ever ate.

III.

Across the way, a gouty nabob dines
His friends with choicest fare and costly wines ;
The table glitters with the wealth of mines.

IV.

On a frail raft, beneath a scorching sky,
Three famished, shipwrecked sailors, with a sigh,
Cast lots to see which one is doomed to die !

TO HENRY WADSWORTH LONGFELLOW.

IN MEMORIAM.

Obiit March 24, 1882.

"*Emigravit* is the inscription on the tombstone where he lies;
Dead he is not, but departed,—for the artist never dies."
"Nuremberg," H. W. LONGFELLOW.

I.

As the swallows, by the wintry winds belated,
  Seek the blooming East to sing their songs of love,
So thy pure and stainless spirit has migrated
  To the beautiful and sunny land above.

There was naught upon this sad earth to detain thee,
  For thy whitening locks were hidden by the bays;
On thy path of flowers there was no thorn to pain thee,
  And thy name was one of reverence and praise.

Thou hast gained the deathless love and the devotion
  Of the millions who have found through thee a goal,
By thy sacerdotal unction and emotion,
  By the purity and sweetness of thy soul.

For within thy most enchanting inspiration
   There forever dwelt a hatred of all wrong ;
And the children came to thee in contemplation,
   As their wonderful and loving Christ of Song !

From our hearts thy cherished name has not departed,
   In imperishable beauty it survives ;
For thy words have healed full many a pain that smarted,
   And thy songs have cast a glamour on our lives.

Every line of thine was like a benediction,
   And could turn our thoughts from sorrow and despair,
While thy voice, when heard in most supreme affliction,
   Was as soothing as the eloquence of prayer.

Thou canst rest in peace, O Poet strong and vernal,
   And rapacious Death for thee has lost his sting,
For thy melodies return to us eternal,
   With the birds, and bees, and blossomings of spring.

Ah, when grief is swift, and haggard are our faces,
   When we hunger, when we thirst for grateful balms,
We can seek and find in thee a safe oasis,
   With a breath of brooks and waving of high palms.

The grand lesson of thy lifetime thou hast taught us,
  The clear sunlight of thy fancy fills our gloom ;
And thy utterance evangelical has brought us
  To believe that all life ends not with the tomb.

II.

When I dream of thee I see in grace and gladness
  The great feudal towers of Nuremberg arise,
Where the rooks, like ghostly messengsrs of sadness,
  Whir their wings above the stone where Dürer lies.

And when weighted down by pain and disaffection,
  When the soul is wrung by many a sorrow keen,
We discover still a hopeful resurrection
  In the deathless faith of thine Evangeline.

Over prairie-flowers there steals thy song mysterious,
  With its scent of golden grain, its pulse of fire,
Hiawatha, with its savage cries imperious,
  With its dreams and dirge, its tumult and desire !

And from clear cathedral chimes thy words come ringing
  Down the lofty halls and highways of the past,
Where the unseen choirs of seraphim are singing,
  When the ruthless fiend is stricken down at last.

'Thou hast summoned up by marvelous necromancy
   The wild sagas of the Northland at thy call,
With the thundering gods, the myths, the rites, the fancy,
   And the banner of Christ refulgent over all.

By thy guiding hand our ravished memory follows
   Thine alluring muse that beckons with a sign,
Through the dreamy glades and fairy-haunted hollows,
   Where the gnomes and elves make revel by the Rhine.

And from many tales and many grave traditions
   Thou hast garnered for our ears a priceless dower ;
And by subtle art and exquisite transitions,
   On these fields of tares thou findest every flower.

O'er dull tomes and scrolls thy master-mind has pondered
   To extract some maxim new for human good,
And with Dante's spirit thou hast gravely wandered
   In the mazes of the dark and sacred wood.

Thou with tenderness hast taught us resignation ;
   Thou hast softened Fate's most pitiless decrees,
And full many a cry of pain and desolation
   Thy delicious, dreamy music can appease !

Thou hast given to dawning youth a new incentive,
    Thou hast cheered the weak and stirred to deeds the strong;
And, oh, sight sublime ! a nation was attentive
    When thy flowers of thought bloomed forth in perfect song!

Ave, poet ! in the Heaven that guides us yonder,
    Ave ! Ave ! noble singer, strong and kind ;
While bereft of thy sweet cadences we wander,
    With thine image in our heart of hearts enshrined.

Thou art gone to join the countless host of shadows,
    But thy sweetness will triumphantly remain,
Like the perfume of the violets on the meadows,
    Made refreshing by the ripple of a rain !

LA MANOLA.

A face of pink and nacker! Tiger eyes,
    Fringed by long, silken lashes black as jet !
    A tortoise-comb high in soft tresses set,
A fan in hand of Oriental dyes,

Screening delicious spheres that fall and rise
    Draped in a frail mantilla's gauzy net.
A satin slipper on a foot that vies
    With Castile's Queen, and which will quickly fret

    When, near the Prado, sounds of castagnette
Of some great revelry or dance apprise.
A vague, strange look of passion you surmise,
    You catch a pleasant scent like mignonette !
She passes ! —— while from sensuous lips there flies
    The blue smoke of her twisted cigarette !

Madrid, 1873.

EXPECTANCY.

When mellow autumn, with its gorgeous blight,
  Blooms grimly death-like among loosened leaves,
I love, poor exile from all earth's delight,
  To seek sad woods on still October eves.

And once, by many a moody thought o'erweighed,
  Wandering, without a definite path or aim,
Unto the weird heart of a gloomy glade,
  Unknown to all my walks, I sudden came.

Blurred by the mists of care, I did not see
  The pall of utter sorrow everywhere,
That seemed to brood upon each dreamy tree
  And haunt the awful quiet of the air.

The broken twigs cracked sharp beneath my tread ;
  No crickets in the grass mad music made ;
The drowsy wood seemed desolately dead ;
  Sepulchral sadness lingered in its shade.

The leaves had long no pleasant breezes known ;
    The birdless boughs for summer seemed to yearn ;
No insects hummed a noisy monotone ;
    No timid squirrel leapt amid the fern.

And as I gazed, in marveling surprise,
    Up through grim branches to the streaks of sky,
The fleet and frightened clouds before my eyes
    Seemed the dark spot to shun, and hurry by.

Then deeper meaning in the solemn shade,
    And colorless, thin grass my fancy found,
As I stood there alone and much afraid,
    Listening in vain for some sweet forest sound.

Such harrowing silence did my sense appall,
    What does this mystery mean ? Is all here dead ?
And as I spoke I saw before me crawl
    A lithe, lean viper, with erected head.

I crushed it in dumb rage, and heard the hell
    Within it hiss me forth malevolence !
The charm was lost ; I gazed about—ah, well!
    Coward I may be, but I hurried hence !

For hideous terror, that can know no balm,
   Dawned on me in the silence of that wood ;
Its grim tranquility, its fearful calm,
   In ways calamitous I understood.

I then knew why it had so strangely slept,
   Bereft of birds, and why no beauteous bloom
Of guileless flowers its intricacies swept,
   While clouds and sunlight shuddered from its gloom.

For it was chosen, alas ! by God on high,
   In his omnipotence supremely grand,
To wildly and most wonderfully die !
   And, when the time did come, His awful hand

Had doomed the fated spot in anger dire
   To feel, with utter horror and dismay,
The *first* annihilating blow of fire
   Warning the world that it was judgment Day !

SONNET.

TO ——.

The vague and vestal beauty of thine eyes
  Recalls the splendor of some Cuban night,
  Where tropic storms, pulsing with golden light,
Hurl dizzy flashes through dark voids of skies !

The trustful look of sweet Actæa lies
  Within their starry depths, that lure and smite
  The souls of men who scorn all woman's might,
And, seeing them, marvel in supreme surprise.

Ah ! when those eyes before me burn and shine
  In soft perfection, I can understand
    White Aphrodite's glance half blurred by foam,
And how Cleopatra, pearl-crowned and divine,
  Gazed upon Antony in her passion grand,
    When for her sake he spurned imperial Rome !

CORONATION.

God took the sapphire of the moaning sea
In His omnipotent hand, mysteriously,

And from the virgin firmaments on high
Seized the immaculate turquoise of the sky.

The livid lightning lumed his passing form,
Grasping the awful ebon of the storm !

And in the labyrinths of space, secrete,
He placed the topaz of the ripening wheat.

The forest and the broad expanse of field
Were called upon their emerald to yield.

And ere the obedient day its task had done,
He plucked the flamant ruby from the sun,

And from the darkness of the brooding night
Ravished the jet that made its holy might.

For rites divine, the mortal may not know,
He tore the iris opal from the bow,

The coral from an angel's lips, and, far
In desolate space, the diamond of a star !

Then, with this matchless wealth before him set,
God made himself an awful coronet !

1877.

CONFIDANTS.

One perfect night, when June lay wrapped in bloom,
  I strolled among the paths of Père La Chaise,
  And, by the cloudless moon's phantasmal rays,
Read the old names on many a grass-wreathed tomb.

Strange moods had lured me to this hallowed gloom,
  And, urged by unknown powers that burn and craze,
  Happy above all men, I sought its ways,
To find, for thoughts exultant, air and room.

I did not dare confide to mortal ear
  The new, sweet bliss that through my spirit spread,
    Nor murmur it in prayer to God above ;—
But I could tell my secret without fear
  To those I pity, the forgotten dead,
    Who have not seen the miracle I love !

ACROSS THE STEPPES.

PART I.

From Nijni, over steppes, I wandered far
  To meet my friend Ivàn Ivànovitch,
  Surnamed in Mohiler, "Ivàn the Rich,"
And drink with him unto our glorious Czar.

The wolves were many on the bleak, drear road,
  But Christus guided with a stainless star
  My frail kibitka where no snowdrifts bar
The deep ruts bending to Ivàn's abode.

With eager arms he came to greet me there:
  " Parlus, my pigeon, thou hast wandered far.
  Enter ! I hear the hissing samovar.
Thou shalt have sterlet and imperial fare.

"The soulless snow shrouds the bare fields in white.
  Sanctus, our reverend Pope, has prophesied
  That until Easter Day will storms abide.
Enter, and sip with me sweet teas this night."

"Ivàn Ivànovitch, thy heart is warm,
 Thy perfect friendship I have much revered ;
 Let me shake off the foam-sleet from my beard,
And I will enter and hide me from the storm."

Then, near his threshold did to me appear,
 In all the glory of emblazoned gold,
 The pure, all-holy image, seraph-souled,
Of his sweet guardian, great St. Vladimir.

"I here salute thy saint and kindly house,"
 I murmured, while he brought me forth a glass
 Filled with a cellar-chilled and creamy quass,
Whispering, "Dear pigeon, drink, the Saint allows."

Then forthwith oaten cakes and caviar,
 Spiced fowl and stchi unto my hand were placed,
 And, until generous warmth the cold effaced,
Silent I watched the hissing samovar.

With many tales I, who had wandered far
 From Astrakhan to Minsk, regaled my friend.
 Of jests and citroned tea there was no end,
And long we drank unto our glorious Czar.

I told Ivàn of gems at Nijni's fair,
  Of far Bokhara, where the Tartar roams,
  And how Archangel's scintillating domes
Tower like gold icebergs in the sunlit air.

Ivàn for me tuned his boleika sweet,
  His songs were soft as angels' when they pray,
  And till the first pale tinge of budding day,
Ballads of love and war we did repeat.

Drowsily listening to the samovar,
  The sleep-god with light pinions touched our eyes:
  Ivàn Ivànovitch, who did early rise;
I, who was worn and who had wandered far.

Calmly we slept, Christus our Lord and Star,
  Communed with pious Vladimir that night,
  And their blunt aureoles, in a cross of light,
Guarded our holy Russia and the Czar.

PART II.

Ivàn Ivànovitch, my pigeon-friend,
  To Nijni, where I held my dwelling, came,
  As often he had promised me, to claim
Shelter, and food, and friendship without end.

The fields were flowerful with an early May
   When, in my garden, by a soft wind fanned,
   I tendered him a hospitable hand
And all my heart, gentle to him alway.

"Pigeon," I said, "the sun on yonder dome
   Has faded many times in peerless grace
   Since I have seen the smile upon thy face ;
Its blesséd radiance now will light my home."

Ivàn gave thanks in accents low and faint,
   Then slowly, reverently, bowed before
   The holy image, guardian of my door,
Katrin the Pure, my Patroness and Saint.

With ravished eyes he gazed on the divine
   And placid face, and murmured in my ear :
   "Pigeon, while *she* doth guard thee, have no fear !
Would, by my village Pope, that she were mine !

" Her hair is golden as the sun-kissed wheat ;
   Her eyes are like the Volga's matchless blue ;
   Those holy lips hold pardon ever new ;
I long to throw my sins before her feet."

"Iuàn Iuànovitch, thou hast wandered far ;
    Saint Katrin will protect thee, dearest guest ;
    Enter within, to chat and take thy rest ;
I hear the hissing of the samovar.

"Long hast thou tarried, like that sacred star,
    That tarried ere its soft, consoling light
    Lit green Judæa's valleys that sweet night,
When Christ was born and shepherds came from far."

My friend Iuàn then lingered by my side,
    And ate my bread and dainty caviar,
    Quaffing strong quass unto our glorious Czar,
Whose valiant deeds are honored far and wide.

Doubtless an evil thought had galled my mind,
    For good Iuàn, whose heart had never changed,
    Seemed in my house, which was his own, estranged ;
And to gay jest his soul was disinclined.

But I remembered he had wandered far,
    That he was worn by many a barren verst ;
    His weariness and voyage I rehearsed
While listening to the hissing samovar.

So I arose and spake: " I leave thee here ;
   Sleep, and may golden dreams delight thine ease,
   I go to rest among my granaries ;
Saint Katrin guards thee, have no evil fear."

When first the dawn with its sweet pulse of light
   Had throbbed thro' darkness to a perfect day,
   Friends came beside my bed, and in dismay
Cried: "Parlus! know'st thou of thy pigeon's flight ?

" With vile intent and sacrilegious hand,
   Soiling thy friendship with ignoble taint,
   He robbed thy house of its protecting Saint,
And with it fled unto another land !

" But ere his feet, detested and accurst,
   Had left domed Nijni town two leagues afar,
   Christus withdrew his kind, protecting star,
And gave unto his soul of deaths the worst.

" Ivàn, thy guest, when shunning thine abode,
   Knew not that gaunt wolves, terror of the town,
   Haunted each dismal wood and lonely down
That leads from here unto the Moscow road.

" His worthless bones upon the holy ground,
   Picked clean and glossy, in the sunlight shine,
   And in his fleshless hand thy Saint divine,
Intact, serene and beautiful, was found."

*   *   *   *   *

Ivàn and I through life had wandered far,
   But Satan tempted my poor pigeon-friend ;
   I often think of his unholy end
When listening to my hissing samovar.

SEVILLE BY MOONLIGHT.

The blue and languorous midnight falls
   Upon Giralda's roseate tower,
Down on the wide, white marble halls,
   Silent and slumberous as the hour.

The air a scent of orange hides,
   The alamedas bloom with balm ;
Where like a thread of silver glides
   The limpid Guadalquivir's calm.

The grand cathedral prays and dreams
   In moonlit quiet, grave and still ;
And every solemn portal teems
   With memories of Moorish skill.

Near, on the plaza, white with stars,
   The indolent majos find repose ;
Around them music of guitars
   Blends with the fragrance of the rose.

A swart gitano loiters by;
　Within his sash the knife sleeps yet :
Bright as the luster of his eye
　Sparkles his twisted cigarette.

A whir of fans half stills a laugh,
　The velvet flash of orbs divine
Reveals fair manolas who quaff
　The golden, rich Montilla wine,

While all the merry groups around,
　Living to love and to forget,
Sing some mad bacchanal of sound,
　Timed by the clicking castanet.

Within the steep and narrow lanes,
　There in the soft and shifting shade,
Float on a song the loves, the pains,
　The languors of the serenade !

And till the warm, sweet night hath flown,
　The dueñas doze, and gallants hope ;
While from faint balconies of stone
　Dangles the tell-tale silken rope.

Hark! through the favoring gloom I hear
  The cautious tread of men that lurk ;
An oath of anger shocks the ear,
  I see the glitter of a dirk.

Waiting above move satined feet,
  Two eyes read passion in two eyes ;
There, in delicious rapture sweet,
  Beauty and youth taste Paradise.

'Tis o'er ! I did not care to wait
  And feel the crimson rain of blood ;
The clash of steel, the groans of hate
  Were long since silenced by the flood

Of song and laughter, clear and loud,
  From gypsies gay who, hand in hand,
A weird, grotesque and brawling crowd,
  Danced a delirious saraband

Until the moon began to wane,
  And with its suite of dreamy stars,
Sank into nothingness again
  Behind the gloom of Alcazars !

THE EARTH SPEAKS.

For years unnumbered I was pure and fair ;
  When God created me to move in space,
  His peerless smile was mirrored in my face,
There was a glory on me everywhere.

My mantle was of flowers and blossoms rare,
  My gardens bloomed with an undying grace ;
  Of dark decay there was no blighting trace,
Death of my bosom's riches had no share.

But then, alas! man in his weakness came,
  Upon me lived and loved, and wept and smiled
    Perishing swiftly as he swiftly spread,
While I, all-pure, to my eternal shame,
  Was by his crowded carrion defiled,
    And filled each day with foul and sheeted dead !

MODJESKA AS "CAMILLE."

Stately, she moves in calm, patrician grace,
　Conscious of power the multitude to thrill !
　While, as a slave, proud Passion at her will
Leaves on her cheek its fiery or tearful trace.

The glooms of anguish dusk her mobile face,
　When cruel words, that maddening thoughts instill,
　Sting, by a prescient sense of future ill,
The new, pure heart that throbs beneath the lace.

But in that sad and agonizing hour,
　When fate relentless taints her perfect dream,
　　And lips that loved insult what they should prize,
It seems as if all Art by her grand power
　Had taken visible shape, to come supreme
　　And gaze upon us from her luminous eyes !

January, 1878.

LOVE SONG.

Oh, my love, on some languorous day,
When the woodlands are dreaming of May,
   And the sky's sapphires gloam thro' them,
With sweet love dawning soft in thine eyes,
Let us seek the green shadows we prize,
   And in ravishment roam thro' them.

Why delay, when the air all around
Is so rare with the gay robin's sound
   And the scent of the tuberose?
Oh, my love, never sun with a light
More supremely, transcendently bright,
   Over Maxos or Cuba rose!

Warm with passion and burning with love,
We will watch the white clouds pass above,
   While the amorous minutes fly,
And will see on the elm's haughty crest,
The frail, beautiful moss-woven nest
   Where at twilight the linnets fly.

On my lips that are parched with desire,
Oh, my love, with their redolent fire,
   Let thy kisses fall manna-like,
While I gaze from the depths of my soul
On thy bosom, voluptuous goal,
   And thy beauty Diana-like!

AN EPISODE OF WATERLOO.

(*Composed in free meter for recitation.*)

The battle was waning, the sun had set
  Thro' the clouds of smoke on the shrieking plain,
And the shattered bodies of men lay wet
  In great pools of blood and great pools of rain.

The thunders of cannon still rent the air,
  And the crimson field had been barely won,
While echoes of anguish drowned the blare
  And greeted the answer of brave Cambronne.

Thro' the dusk and gloom from the north advanced,
  With helmeted heads and vigorous breath,
The dragoons of Blücher, equipped and lanced,
  To swell the red tides of the river Death.

And the Emperor stood on the gory field,
  With his great, calm eyes in a strange unrest,
But his forehead's pale marble ne'er revealed
  All the burning hell in his tortured breast.

It was o'er, and the victor's eager cry
   Rose up in the night, while the piercing groans
Of thousands of heroes left to die
   Blent shrill with the cannon's monotones.

Thro' the heat of fire, thro' the bullets' rain,
   Thro' the sea of battle that stormed and waved,
The pale man on the prancing horse again
   Led his legions on, for France might be saved.

And though all seemed lost, *he* was still adored
   By those valorous hearts that knew naught of fear,
And the maimed and dying, with limbs begored,
   As he hurried by would arise and cheer.

*   *   *   *   *   *   *

There was one poor soldier, who lay between
   Five mangled Prussians and heard him pass ;
He surmised him near, for he had not *seen*,
   And he struggled to rise from the bloody grass.

He had left his mother in old Touraine,
   His sister Jeanne and his father blind,
But remembered naught of their love again
   When the thought of his Emperor filled his mind.

He thought, as he wallowed in clotted gore,
    Of the sweetheart he quitted against his will,
Of the dear old home he would see no more,
    But the Emperor held his heart's love still.

His left arm had been shattered by grape and shell
    And hung to the bone by a single thread !
But he heard the great Emperor's voice—and, well,
    " I'll give one last proof of my love," he said.

For he felt that his darling chief was nigh,
    And wrenched the dead arm from the broken blade
And cried with his weak, poor, feeble cry,
    " It has served thee well, and for thee 'twas made !"

And he waved it high in his frantic might
    As Napoleon passed with a flash and whir,
And his last words rang through the awful night :
    "*Vive l'Empereur! Vive l'Empereur!*"

1874.

HUITZILOPOTCHLI.

Great in the gory grandeur of thy palace,
      God over war and din !
Thy grave eyes glitter in a sullen malice
        On foe and kin
        And all who sin.
Thou waitest tranquil near thy teocallis,
Grim in thy stone, erect, austere and callous,
    Until the sacrificial rites begin.

Thou seem'st to smile and hear the approaching thrumming
      Of lutes that hail the feast ;
The serpent-skins sob with the angry drumming
        Of slave and priest,
        While, e'er increased,
The trembling crowds like bees in swarms are humming,
As from the distant, fair chinampas coming,
    They drag their palsied victims, man and beast.

High on the dizzy altar-green thou standest,
          Lit by the sacred fire ;
Huitzilopotchli ! god of gods, our grandest,
          Serene and dire !
          In might and ire
O'er tzin, and slave, and peon thou commandest,
And when in wrath thou haughtily expandest,
     Vast, shuddering throngs to grant thy whims aspire.

The human hearts that reek upon thy altar,
          Oh, wondrous god, are ours !
Our flesh and souls by thy decrees ne'er falter ;
          We bless thy dowers,
          When crimson showers
Of the fierce foe, the arrogant assaulter,
Fall at thy feet ; for thy celestial halter
     Is soft unto our necks, oh, god of powers !

Our lives before thy glance are weak and brittle,
          Like thinnest slits of slate
When smitten by the iron maquahuitl.
          Oh, god, abate
          Thy scorn irate.
Oh, master of the sweet Ixtlilxochitl,
Of thy great balm, waft on our heads a little
     To cheer and solace our poor brows prostrate !

Around thy feet, oh, mighty god, and under
    The sacred odors steal
Of clotted gore from bosoms torn asunder,
    Of limbs that reel !
    Oh, bless our zeal,
And o'er the cries and frenzied groans of wonder
Of those tormented hurl thy angry thunder
    To drown their agonizing last appeal.

The white and demon foe have ta'en our cattle,
    And yet we do not sigh!
We have no food, no fruit, no cacao-latl.
    The hours pass by :
    Oh, lord most high,
Lend us thy strength to struggle in the battle,
And thro' the clash of arms when lances rattle
    To bring thee other victims ere we die !

Our arms are strong, our bows are long and slender,
    Our knives are curved and clear,
Our maquahuitls find the foes' flesh tender.
    Oh, god, appear !
    Superb ! Severe !
To guide us onward in a cloud of splendor,
And o'er the carrion of the vile offender
    Our songs of praise, exultant, thou shalt hear.

Thy fearful anger sleeps, alert! awake it!
   And in thy proud disdain
Cleave with thy lance the Christian spell and break it.
    Our arrows' rain
    Now falls in vain.
If thou hast thirst, their veins were made to slake it.
Thy people swoons, oh, god, do not forsake it
   Now, in this hour of servitude and pain!

Consume with fire, with pest and desolation,
    Stern Cortez and his band!
Harrow his pagan soul with war's vexation!
    Thou, ever grand,
    Stretch forth thine hand,
Strong and immutable for our salvation!
Sustain the Tzin Guatamo and the nation,
   Save Tenochtitlan and our holy land!

PASTEL.

Among the priceless gems and treasures rare
  Old Versailles shelters in its halls sublime,
I can recall one faded image fair,
  A girl's sad face, praised once in every clime.

Poets have sung, in rich and happy rhyme,
  Her violet eyes, the wonder of her hair.
An art-bijou it was, but dimmed by time,
  A dreamy pastel of La Vallière !

I, too, remember in my heart a face
  Whose charm I deemed would ever with me dwell
But as the days went by, its peerless grace
  Fled like those dreams that blooming dawn dispel,
Till of its beauty there was left no trace,
  Time having blurred it like that pale pastel !

LATHAM CORNELL STRONG.

DIED DECEMBER, 1879.

Grim death has hushed the soft, melodious sound
   That filled thy spirit, and the vital flame,
     Engendering noble thoughts that graced thy name,
Is spent, while dismal ashes strew the ground.

Thy worshiped muse with thee in plenty found
   Delicious charm and beauty without blame ;
     Yet, while thy laurels were prepared by Fame,
Thou didst not wait to be supremely crowned !

Oh, pious pilgrim in the paths of art,
   Thy gentle labor has not been in vain,
     Exalting excellence, combating wrong !
For all thy words were warm unto the heart,
   And ere thy days were done men saw thee gain
     The rare and radiant Mecca of sweet song !

THE CARP AT ST. GERMAIN.
1515 — 1881.

(A carp died in a pond at St. Germain in 1881. A thin plate of gold had been fastened to its gill by Francis First, King of France.)

The brave and manly form of Francis First,
  When I was young, in reverence I saw
Stooping to slake his fierce and royal thirst,
  Encompassed by his silent suite in awe.

Beside him stood, obedient to his call,
  The merry Triboulet, his feathered fool,
Who aped his gracious majesty in all
  And deeply drank the water of my pool.

While the grim Spanish despot by his side,
  The haughty and all-sacred monarch Charles,
Threw me some crumbs in his Castilian pride,
  Hushing his perfumed lap-dogs' envious snarls.

I see as if no time had passed since then,
  Since those dead epochs of great deeds and sins,
The knights, and cavaliers, and lordly men
  Who came to watch the flashing of my fins.

And I recall the merry and sunny day
  When Catherine, the withered Queen in black,
Gazed on my silver loveliness at play,
  And how from her stern stare I glided back.

Ay ! and I see again, like some bright star
  Of beauty in the heaven's eternal blue,
The peerless glance of Margaret of Navarre
  Piercing the ripples that I wandered through.

Bussy, the brave, has given me golden cake,
  When mute he pondered on his many loves ;
And the vile *mignons* who, with envy ache,
  Tossed me their sugared fruit and scented gloves.

And in their wake the anointed Henri came,
  Poodle-escorted and in folly sunk ;
While near him stood, with greedy eyes of flame,
  Clutching a dirk, the lean, avenging monk !

Ah ! happier were the days when Gabrielle
  Fed me with the lithe beauty of her hands ;
While the great King, good Harry, we loved well,
  Fought for the glory of our fertile lands.

She passed before me like a radiant dream ;
   And then I saw a feeble man, unknown,
Albeit a King, with Richelieu, supreme,
   Sneering in red, while crumbs were to me thrown.

And there, alert, stood, smiling by his side,
   Armed to the teeth, a hero without fear,
Bold D' Artagnan in all his Gascon pride,
   The beau-ideal of a musketeer !

Alas ! Death's harvest in those days was great.
   They lingered but a span.   Then to me came
The august Louis, in his powdered state,
   And sweet La Vallière with soft eyes of shame.

And with him walked strange people, clad in black,
   Yet affable and seeming foes to care,
Who gravely smiled behind the kingly back,
   And had odd names, like Boileau and Molière.

Then, after lapses of eventless time,
   The languid witchery of la Pompadour
Drew me in rapture from my bed of slime,
   And to her hand my shyness did allure.

While near her, simple servant to her nod,
  With smiles and glances that no scorn could tire,
Stood, beautiful and haughty as a god,
  The pale young monarch, trembling with desire.

Alas ! he, too, forgot her beauty soon,
  Such is the destiny of love's eclipse,
For when he came again, the summer moon
  Silvered his kisses on Du Barry's lips.

Then I beheld, bent down by many woes,
  A Cæsar-browed humiliated Queen,
While in the traitorous town afar arose
  The crimson horror of the guillotine.

And once in agony of fear I heard
  Atrocious blasphemies pollute the air,
And many an odious, God-defying word
  Thundered by Danton and by Robespierre.

They passed, and I for days was left alone.
  Strange noises of the city came from far ;
No dainty morsels in my waves were thrown ;
  The sky was burning like a fiery star.

Then passed a man whose brow was white and great,
　　As awful God himself, come here below,
Marked by the calm serenity of Fate,
　　The man of Jéna and of Montereau !

But foes united, hundreds against one,
　　Crushed by brute force amid the cannon's roar,
His valorous eagles flying to the sun,
　　And he, the mighty emperor, came no more.

Then fertile peace showered blessings on the land ;
　　Gross, idle kings held shackled Paris down,
And near my fountain-brink would often stand
　　Men greater far than warriors of renown.

I watched kind Gautier's fascinating smile,
　　And Hugo's grave communion with the muse ;
Pale Lamartine, who cherished nothing vile,
　　And Musset dreaming of his Andalouse.

And then with powder and the barricade
　　The second empire sullenly began ;
While the new monarch passed, in gold arrayed,
　　The trembling shadow of the Lodi man !

But mirth and merriment were with him, too.
   In routs and revels he was not alone ;
While cannon roared and many banners blew
   To hail the splendor of his phantom throne.

And when barbaric hosts in steel again
   Sallied, my beauteous gardens passing by,
I shrank into my bed of weeds in pain,
   Wearied by centuries, and glad to die !

THE SECRET.

I sang with rapture to the passing breeze
My dawning love's supremest mysteries,
With the soft rhymes of passion beautified.
The graceful melody spread far and wide ;
And as my song was soothing as a prayer,
The kind breeze lingered in the drowsy air,
And when the long confession had been heard,
I softly whispered it unto a bird,
A wee, brown robin on a willow tree,
That relished all and made great sport of me.
Fearing the precious scandal might pass by,
I told it to the brilliant butterfly ;
Which, idly dallying 'mid the dewy flowers,
Thro' the long, dreamy, languid summer hours,
Straightway flew off to prattle of my woes,
My hopes and sweet ambition, to the rose ;
Which, having heard the loving words I said,
Blushed in delight a purer, deeper red,
And rashly vowed within its crimson core
To keep and treasure them forevermore.

But, like a luminous star of love and light,
The one I loved chanced to pass there that night,
And gently plucked the dainty rose to share
The silken splendors of her wavy hair.
And then the mystery I held so dear
Must have been tempted from the rose, I fear,
For, though I surely had no subtle part,
My secret fluttered to her ravished heart,
And, like a dove that finds its shelter fair,
Lovingly, confidently nestled there,
Until its burden, longing to be free,
Escaping from her lips flew back to me!

THE NAUTCH GIRL.

Her limbs are lithe and supple as the sea ;
   Jet hair in perfumed waves is windward whirled ;
   And, below tinted lashes, crisp and curled,
Her gold-black glances glitter like a bee !

Graceful and flexile as the desert tree,
   Her frame voluptuous, sapphire-starred and pearled,
   Slips in dusk radiance from its veil unfurled,
A luring vision of guile and ecstasy.

A Rajah's ransom glistens on a breast
   Burning with ardor as the timbrels boom ;
   And cruel eyes flash fire into the gloom,
Stirring the senses to a vague unrest ;
   While, in her pagan passion uncontrolled,
   Her dreams are red like blood and bright like gold !

March 18, 1887.

AWAKENING.

How terrible that fugitive moment seems,
　　When tortured minds, steeped in serenest sleep,
Awaken from the ravishment of dreams
　　Only to recollect their woes and weep !

Now, when the grim realities of pain
　　Dawn in vague, solemn ways within their breast,
They fain would lull their sense to slumber again,
　　And shun the odious light that brings no rest !

In that brief, harrowing second some recall
　　The pitiless fate that o'er their path has crossed ;
In their friendly sleep they have forgotten all ;
　　They wake, alas ! to mourn a loved one lost !

Some mother, worn by vigils and by care,
　　With sweet, fallacious visions now beguiled,
Smiling, awakes and, ere she is aware,
　　Calls by some pretty name her darling child !

But he is dead ; and, ah! her many tears
   Rebel against sleep's suave, delusive power ;
Better the anguish of continual fears
   Than the false promise of that cruel hour !

Perchance some maiden of her winning grace
   Dreams, while no troublous thought disturbs her ease.
She wakes, and then remembers the pale trace
   Stamped on her beauty by some fierce disease.

The wounded soldier, tossing on his bed,
   Has visions of glory and of valorous strife.
He wakes and with convulsive chills of dread
   Now recollects his limbs are lost for life.

The contrite murderer in his damp, drear cell
   Dreams that he hears some merciful angel say :
"God hath thy crimes forgiven, all is well."
   He wakes, and knows he will be hanged that day.

O, bounteous sleep ! Restorer of the mind !
   When poor souls suffer from misfortune's sting,
Whisper to Death, thy brother, grave and kind :
   "Spare them the agony of awakening !"

1877.

TO LOUIS BLUMENBERG, VIOLONCELLIST.

The soul that lingers in the silent strings
　　Rises in rhythmic magic by thy hand,
　　A tuneful vassal e'er at thy command,
A soul invisible that weeps or sings

Melodious strains, like passing angels' wings,
　　Seem from the speaking maple to be fanned
　　While graver meaning, mystical and grand,
A matchless grace unto our senses brings.

Ah! when those strains fall gently on my ear,
I breathe in ravishment and seem to hear
　　Seraphic choirs that worship and adore,
And I, a skeptic, marveling in surprise,
Feel wondrous tears of pity fill my eyes,
　　And, penitent, believe in God once more.

December 11, 1884

KING TO FAVORITE.

My stately modern towns are strangely cold ;
  Their hybrid architecture, dull and tame,
Lacks pearls, and Paros, and symmetric gold
  To set thy beauty in a worthy frame.

I dream for thee of svelt Greek colonnades,
  Or glorious Parthenons, where statues gleam
Amid the flowery urns and frail arcades,
  And like a musing army of marble seem.

I dream of marvelous granite cities, where,
  Guarded by sphinxes in eternal calm,
Tall obelisks pierce the blue and cloudless air
  Above parterres of lotus and of palm.

Fit for thy home, I see, near Amoy's skies,
  Great kaolin kiosks and weird pagodas glow,
Bedragoned flags, idols with ruby eyes,
  And quaint junks gliding down the Hoang-ho.

Or yet, Ind's monstrous temples to Vischnû,
  Where gods with elephantine faces stand,
And where, in Kief, ecstatic thou canst view
  The inhuman rites, the lawless saraband.

I build for thee, beneath Granada's stars,
  Poems of stone, with Mihrâbs in their heart,
Supreme Alhambras, lofty Alcazars,
  One arabesque of Saracenic art!

But, ah! these earthly splendors, everywhere,
  Pass in my dreams, imperfect, undefined,
For I would have thy peerless beauty share
  The unbuilt Romes and Karnacs of my mind.

1877.

TO A SCRAP OF SEA-WEED.

Neglected flower that in the ocean blooms,
　　Poor exile from the fragrant groves of earth,
What sorrow rises in thy salt perfumes,
　　To what sad thoughts thy humble charm gives birth !

Tossed by the tempest and fluctuant tide,
　　The vulgar plaything of the slimy eel ;
Crushed by the vessel's keel or cast aside,
　　What bitterness thy injured heart must feel !

Thy lovely sisters blush on field and lawn,
　　The lily, pink and rose are kin to thee,
Yet thou art destined, from grim night till dawn,
　　To hide thy envy in the turbulent sea.

Alas ! none know why thou wast strangely torn
　　From leafy woodlands and rich orchards blest,
Nor why thou shouldst not have been sweetly born
　　A tuberose to grace my darling's breast,

Unless the Eternal, in His august might,
 A sacred usage for thy beauty found,
And made thee to fulfill some sacred rite
 Upon the ghastly foreheads of the drowned.

THE FALSE LOVER.

I love thee as the wild bees love the South,
  When May has made the broad savannas fair ;
I love the roses of thy perfect mouth,
  And all the redolent summer of thy hair.

Thou art the Mecca of my pilgrim soul,
  The peerless dawn that floods my spirit's night ;
Thou art my consolation and my goal,
  My ravishment, my solace, my delight !

Lift thy veiled eyes and scan the heavens afar,
  Far in those blue immensities, and see
That radiant and imperishable star,
  Pure as my deathless worship is for thee.

Why dost thou start, oh ! my delicious love ?
  What cruel fantasy thy soul appalls ?
Oh, God ! Oh, God ! cast not thy eyes above,
  The warning star in trails of silver falls !

J. S. THEBAUD.

IN MEMORIAM.

I.

To a World unworthy, full of pride and peril,
  Thou hast given, as would a god, thy better part;
And upon its obdurate bosom, stern and sterile,
  Thou hast sown the sweetest lilies of thy heart.

Thou hast built to Duty a new and sumptuous altar,
  Thou hast baffled Death upon its gloomiest porch;
And with firm, progressive hand that could not falter,
  Thou hast held through densest night thy science-torch!

Without power divine, thy gentle touch caressing
  Checked the spreading seeds of danger and decay;
And, as lepers went to Christ for balm and blessing,
  Thy afflicted poor would come to thee and pray.

Thou hast not, like haughty kings, a throne or palace,
  And there gleamed no crown of rubies on thy brows;
But no human pain found thy great spirit callous,
  And no chagrin unallayed e'er left thy house.

As the expectant shepherds in Judæa's valley
  Rose to follow one bright, luminous star divine,
So disconsolate hosts of sufferers would rally
  And find solace in the glory that was thine.

From a monument of Hope beamed forth thy cresset ;
  All around Death fluttered cold wings through the air ;
But the pestilential chill could not repress it,
  Nor dissuade thy sheltered ones from lingering there.

Thou hast braved life's taunts and bitterness unfailing,
  Yet thy will hath never trembled at the shock ;
For, erect and firm, its blows were unavailing
  To destroy thy Faith's invulnerable rock.

II.

As some mighty oak, assailed by storms outdaring,
  Mourns in vain its blighted boughs and scattered leaves,
So my heart, in deepest trials of despairing,
  Mourns thy vanished smile on these sad winter eves.

As the rose regrets the golden summer's splendor,
  As the lark recalls with woe its absent mate,
So my soul regrets thy kindnesses most tender,
  So my thought recalls thy virtues strong and great.

As the shipwrecked sailor, struggling with wild billows
　　On some fragile spar, and to destruction tossed,
Sadly yearns for his far home and village willows,
　　So my stricken spirit yearns for what is lost.

Thou art gone, but, ah ! the bitter, bitter anguish !
　　What have feeble words to sing thy value done?
Thou art gone, alas ! and left us here to languish,
　　Like some dooméd planet without hope or sun.

For we miss thy winning ways and joyous greeting,
　　Thy bright, laughing eye, thy warm, responsive hand,
As some wrinkled exile, waiting and entreating,
　　Ever misses his dear tyrant-haunted land.

Can the songs of bards in most supreme affliction,
　　Can the silent grief, or grief with cheeks beteared,
Can the humble prayer, or churchly benediction,
　　Bring thee back to us, pale shadow we revered ?

What are sobs of woe and dews upon the forehead,
　　What are outward signs of pitiless pang and smart,
When compared with the relentless, stern, all horrid,
　　Strong and speechless torment of a desolate heart ?

What strange tears were those shed on the mausoleums
  Of historic conquerors since the world was young !
Seems there not a sound of battle in their Te Deums ?
  Seems there not hot blood on every singer's tongue ?

If such scourges by vile multitudes were petted,
  If cowed nations mourned such evanescent powers,
What must be the pain of men who have regretted
  One great worthy soul, whose memory is ours ?

Mother Earth, though grave and mute, is no despiser
  Of the few and noble sons that are her own ;
And the world, by her grand prompting voice grown wiser,
  Will recall thy name when Cæsar's is unknown.

III.

As the pliant palm, above the desert towering,
  Blooms in utter fear of some hot, mad simoom,
So my groping mind, in dismal darkness cowering,
  Dreads to lift the awful shadow from thy tomb.

Can our faith in some sweet future life supernal
  Cope with gnawing doubt, and all its vigor keep,
When we know our separation is eternal
  On this hateful sphere, whose only balm is sleep ?

No! The vials of wrath hold no more tribulation ;
   There must be some cruel limit to all pain ;
Still we dream of thee in all our desperation,
   As a withering violet dreameth of the rain.

From no Bible, or no Koran, can we borrow
   Consolation for the ravage Death has done ;
And we long for thee thro' suffering and thro' sorrow,
   As the polar night longs for the absent sun.

Like our mother's kiss, and like our youth's fond gladness,
   Like our perished hopes, and like our boyish fears,
Like our first-born love, half passion and half sadness,
   We regret thee through the long and weary years.

And, oh ! noble friend, for whom all pain has ended,
   I salute with my poor, melancholy song,
Thy unsullied life, wherein all virtues blended,
   Thy superior mind, 'mid danger ever strong.

I salute thy memory, I, the latest comer,
   And I mourn thy dolorous loss, uncomforted,
As the brown, bare fields salute the dying summer,
   As the warm heart mourns when love is doomed and dead.

December, 1876.

THE SPHINX SPEAKS.

Carved by a mighty race whose vanished hands
    Formed empires more destructible than I,
    In sultry silence I forever lie,
Wrapped in the shifting garment of the sands.

Below me, Pharaoh's scintillating bands
    With clashings of loud cymbals have passed by,
    And the eternal reverence of the sky
Falls royally on me and all my lands.

The record of the future broods in me ;
    I have with worlds of blazing stars been crowned,
      But none my subtle mystery hath known
Save one, who made his way through blood and sea,
    The Corsican, prophetic and renowned,
      To whom I spake, one awful night alone !

AN IDYL OF PROVENCE.

With Love's aurora beaming in their eyes,
    Mute and enraptured, going hand in hand,
They slowly wander through the paradise
    Of their green, golden, blossom-haunted land.

Their footsteps fade in mazes of soft ferns,
    The sunny air is languorous with flowers,
And in the distance, where the blue Rhone turns,
    They see their vine-wreathed homes and trysting bowers.

The changeless azure of the autumn sky
    Showers all its glory on the enamored pair,
While the glad southern breezes gently sigh
    Amid the tangle of the maiden's hair.

Her heart, as blithe as songs of summer birds,
    Sees life sun-colored now, without eclipse ;
Her fond glance thrills him, and delicious words
    Part the warm scarlet of her perfect lips.

The beauty of antique Arles, wine-tinged and Greek,
  Seems in her fluttering breast to grandly live ;
And in shy ways she fain would claim and seek
  The kisses, long deferred, he fain would give.

He tells her in the glow of youth and pride,
  With winning words, a murmur and a fire,
How to this hour, supreme and sanctified,
  His timid soul did never dare aspire.

He tells how all his love with fears did cope,
  And how from doubt and dream it nobly grew
To this sweet resurrection of dead hope,
  To this felicity, divine and true.

Then, from his buoyant heart, elate, sincere,
  He whispers all that Love holds pure and rare,
Persuasive incoherences made dear,
  And accents tender as a vestal's prayer.

While she, whose spirit is won and fails to speak,
  Gazes upon him in a charmed surprise,
With deepening roses on each burning cheek,
  And all the trust of heaven within her eyes.

THE WITNESS.

They tell me that I never loved the fair,
    Delicious maid, who now in endless sleep
    Can charm the grave ; because I do not weep,
And shriek to the cold world my great despair.

They say my heart of gentle ruth is bare
    As leafless trees, and that I do not keep
    Her memory sacred, while, sincere and deep,
That heart is haunted by her everywhere !

Alas ! how can I prove ? Oh ! beauty mine,
    Wrapped in grim cerements, how refute them now ?
    Would couldst thou rise and tell my love unique.
But I am helpless without guide or sign :
    The silent moon alone has heard my vow : —
        Damn thee, white, senseless thing ! Wilt thou not speak?

GIANTS AND GRUBS.

*" Il n'y a que les petits esprits qui constatent les imperfections des chefs-
d' œuvre.—*VOLTAIRE.

When will the shades of great men rest in peace
    And be revered, as they deserve, on earth?
When will the mongrel horde of scoffers cease
    To harm their memory and denounce their worth?

Will the Greek symmetry of their perfect thought
    Be ever ravaged by these modern Huns?
Can naught restrain these lesser beings, fraught
    With bitter hatred for dead, mighty ones?

Shall impotent critics, balked of fleeting fame,
    In envious wrath lay down Draconian law,
Turning to ridicule some noble name
    That shows a brilliant diamond's lightest flaw?

Yet the world listens to their noisome words,
    Harks to their puerile rage and malcontent;
While they, like ignorant migrating birds,
    Would soil a Phidias with their excrement!

An easy task, forsooth!   Delicious themes,
    To sneer at what is grand, and pure, and far;
But, to my eyes, their mad persistence seems
    Like some pale fire-fly jealous of a star.

And when I see these pompous creatures strut,
    And note the paltry mischief they have done,
I smile, and think of some foul Lapland hut
    That might be envious of a Parthenon!

THE ANDALUSIAN SERENO.

With oaken staff and swinging lantern bright,
   He strolls at midnight when the world is still,
Through dismal lanes and plazas plumed with light,
   Guarding the drowsy thousands in Seville.

Gazing upon his ever star-thronged sky,
   With careless step he wanders to and fro ;
The gloomy streets re-echo with his cry,
   His slow, low, sad and dreary " *Se-re-no !* "

He sees the blonde moon fleck the rosy towers
   Of old Giralda with its opal sheen,
And in broad alamedas, warm with flowers,
   He sees the Moorish cypress bend and lean.

Then, vaguely dreaming, he recalls the nights
   His father passed beneath those very stars,
The tales of escaladed walls, the fights,
   The mirth, the songs, the Babel of guitars !

And all his sire had told him years ago,
    How, often, in the gardens dim and dark,
He met full many a mantled Romeo,
    And stumbled over corpses cold and stark.

But he, alas ! had heard no serenade ;
    No ladder hangs from Donna Linda's bars,
And the wan glint of an assassin's blade
    He ne'er has seen beneath these quiet stars.

So, weary, in the dead calm of the town,
    His soul regrets the Past's romantic glow,
While mute, despondent, pacing up and down,
    He sadly moans his dreary "*Se-re-no !*"

But sometimes in the grayish light of dawn
    He stops and trembles in his clinging cape,
For he can see a lady's curtain drawn,
    And, in the street below, a phantom shape.

Draped in quaint, antique garb, with sword and glove,
    Sombrero vast, and mandolin on arm,
Which seems to play a weird, wild lay of love,
    And at his coming shows no quick alarm ;

But turns, and there a skeleton, all lean
   And haggard, leers within the lightless lane !
And the Sereno knows that he has seen
   The specter of the Past, the ghost of Spain !

CONTRASTS.

I.—PAGANISM (?)

Rome B. C.

A thousand temples! silver! marble! gold!
  A revel of color and a feast of art!
  Immortal poets! a stupendous mart!
Victorious legends! pageantry untold!

Man against beast! the gladiators bold,
  The mangled tiger and the bleeding heart,
  The roars of lions groaning by the dart,
And over all the banner of Rome unrolled!

Trophies of distant wars! mad crowds a-glee!
  A thunder of plaudits bursting o'er the town!
  Conquest and splendor! glory and renown!
And near the Coliseum I can see,
  Above the clarion-throated, seething mass,
  Great laureled Cæsar to the Forum pass!

II.— CIVILIZATION (?)

Third Avenue at Night.

Foul, heated houses in a garbaged street !
  Great, shrieking locomotives rattling by !
  The stench of cess-pools rising to the sky ;
Squalor and horror ! rottenness effete !

Coarse rabble-crowds rush by, all sins to greet :
  Money and lust is their perpetual cry,
  While near the lamps the musky cyprians sigh,
And lechery and filth hold power complete !

Great gangs of tramps and ruffians unclean,
  Ignoble panders to all vice and slime,
    Parade amid the rush of dirty cars,
Or hold in corners minglements obscene ;
  While passing, gorged with beer and ripe for crime,
    Gross Germans bellow at the holy stars !

July, 1887.

AUSTERLITZ.

On the broad field of Austerlitz I passed
  And watched, one wintry day, along its moor
Thin flakes of snow fall silently and fast,
  Like powdered marble, flocculent and pure.

The incoherent murmur of the breeze
  Sounded like ghostly drum-taps to my ear,
While on the gaunt, bare, tempest-stricken trees,
  The shivering whir of bird-wings I could hear.

My timorous guide, awed by an unknown dread,
  Had left me pathless in these icy glooms,
Alone in this last bivouac of the dead,
  Alone amid innumerable tombs!

Pensive I gazed upon the drear expanse
  Where the Titanic struggle had been won,
And where the legions of Imperial France
  Acclaimed the genius of Napoleon!

And then before me phantom visions soared
   Of men blood-maddened, hurrying to the fray ;
Again the deep-lunged, angry cannon roared,
   Hailing the victory of that fearful day !

I heard again the conqueror's voice supreme,
   The shrill, sharp echo of the trumpet's blare,
When horses plunge, and gory sabers gleam
   In one red revel of immense despair !

The fury of fancy took me by surprise
   And hurled me in the dread fight's hottest glow ;
But when I lifted up my eager eyes
   Naught greeted them but wastes of solemn snow !

Over the graves with bones heroic filled
   By one who for ambition greatly sinned,
I only heard, while all my senses thrilled,
   The mournful misereres of the wind !

And as I passed in dreary monotone,
   Thro' groups of desolate pine and leafless fir,
It seemed to me in agony to moan
   Vague, dismal sounds like "*vive l' Empereur!*"

SOUVENIR.

Like a Sultana clad in raiment bright,
  Voluptuous Provence, draped in olive trees,
  Balmy with grain and the soft southern breeze,
Dreamed to the star-thronged heaven one perfect night.

It seemed as if our God had made the site
  His rare and unique fantasy to please,
  And for his wonders and his mysteries
Created it from roses, calm and light !

'T was there — sweet spot ! — where thy ripe lips divine,
  In passionate embrace — oh ! long-craved boon ! —
    Placed their soft, troubled warmth unto my own ;
'T was there that thou wert mine, that I was thine ;
  While over us the autumn-mellow moon
    Silvered the languorous ripples of the Rhone !

PROOF.

The world shrieks "atheist" in my face, and cries:
  "How canst thou the Eternal God aggrieve?
Why doubt? He made the earth, the stars, the skies,
  And thy vile dust! Yet thou wilt not believe!"

For answer I seek the woman whom I prize,
  One who can rule me by her slightest nod,
And as I gaze in her calm, treacherous eyes,
  Convinced, I sigh, *there can not be a God!*

JEBEL - AL - TARIK.

GIBRALTAR.

A giant captive, I command
The entrance to Hispania's strand;
A foreign flag above me floats,
My flanks are girt by foreign boats,
Inviolate I may remain,
But all my spirit is with Spain.

In the warm Andalusian sun
I dream of the brave deeds undone;
I watch my rightful owners pass,
With eyes averted, and, alas!
Although they merit my disdain,
My love and hope are still with Spain.

The red - coats on my haughty brow
Pass stern and silent, even now;
While in the fertile plains below
The idle Spaniards come and go.
To claim their rights they do not deign;
But still my spirit burns for Spain.

JEBEL-AL-TARIK.

She has no hosts of valiant knights,
In armor clad, to scale my heights;
There is no Cid Campeador
To drive the stranger from my shore,
With flash of swords and fiery rain;
But still my spirit yearns for Spain.

The days of valorous deeds have passed,
And chivalry is dead at last.
I see proud England's haughty fleet
Hover in safety at my feet;
There is no blood to wash my stain;
But still my heart is warm for Spain.

Ah! better far the glorious years
When Caliphs, flanked by Moslem spears,
Fought on my terraces like men.
Spain nursed a race of heroes then;
To humble me foes sought in vain;
For all my spirit was with Spain.

I can recall with pride immense
The rows of Saracenic tents,
When Tarik dwelt upon my breast,
Protected by the Moorish crest;

I saw his legions dot the plain;
But all my heart was true to Spain.

I, too, recall when Guzman came
In silk and steel, in smoke and flame;
The flag of Christ on high he waved;
My walls with Moorish blood he laved;
No danger could his hand restrain;
And all my soul was proud of Spain.

Again the fierce Moors to me thronged,
And to their sovereign I belonged;
While, warring with a Christian zeal,
I saw Alfonso of Castile
Die near his myriads of slain;
And all my soul went forth to Spain.

Then came the hated men in red,
For massacre and pillage bred;
In lines I marked their swift advance
Against the chivalry of France.
Alas! the battle was their gain;
But still my heart believed in Spain.

They came in shouting bands, like Huns,
And armed me with their thousand guns ;
They filled my arcades, dark and dumb,
With the loud rattle of the drum ;
They trampled down the summer grain
And bade defiance to my Spain.

Ah ! how much longer must I stand
A captive in my holy land ?
Will no Manrique arise to drag,
Through blood and mire, that crimson flag?
Must I live on in silent pain
And learn to lose my love for Spain ?

Ah ! no ; the future brighter seems ;
Prophetic visions fill my dreams ;
For there shall come a day of pride
When I, with Spaniards at my side,
Shall thunder from my guns again
My loyal, deathless love for Spain !

1882.

TO ERNESTO ROSSI, IN "HAMLET."

Could glorious Shakespeare walk the earth again,
   Right merrily would he laugh at all the toil
   Of men bespangled, who forever soil
His perfect "Hamlet," marvel of his brain.

Yea, he would smile at their insensate Dane,
   Who, of his genius, was the proudest spoil.
   From all their frowns and groans he would recoil,
And his great ghost would reason and complain.

But, if he knew thee, Rossi, he would cry,
   "I see my 'Hamlet'; yea, the one I love
   Within my spirit's depths.   I see the goal
Of my own mind that is not born to die,
   And find in *thine* the thought which God above
   Gave to the deathless essence of my soul!"

November 8, 1881.

IHLANG - IHLANG.

The gold Hoang-ho lulls with fluctuant tide
   The marble palace of the Mandarin ;
   Without bloom citron-gardens, and within
Rise stately court-yards, porticoed and wide.

I hear of tinkling bells the silver din
   From porcelain towers, whence caracole and ride
   Great hosts of Mongols, while from Han-tung's side
The annual festivals with pomp begin.

Ravished I see a lithe, sweet, doe-eyed girl,
   Che-Kiang's most sacred princess, passing through
The merry town where dragoned flags unfurl
   Their gold and argent on her hair's dusk hue ;
I see her enter, catch her smile of pearl,
   And smell a wondrous perfume, strange and new !

HERO AND TRAITOR.

I.

Upon the confines of the Promised Land
Two radiant seraphim forever stand,

Guarding with flaming swords and tireless eyes
The abode of heroes in God's paradise.

Here the Eternal, in omnipotence,
Ordains for them a lasting recompense.

But few, alas ! in history's pages known,
Can claim this perfect Eden for their own.

But many are there whose names no rosters show,
Spirits from Lodi's sun, from Moscow's snow.

Relicts of Ivry and the perished brave
Of Wagram's flame or Navarino's wave.

Heroes of every race, of every creed —
All who were valorous in the heart and deed.

II.

Before Marengo's field was won in blood,
A wounded ghost before the angels stood,

Whose august brow, republican, severe,
Stamped him as one that never knew a fear.

With humble voice, unconscious of his fate,
He craved admittance at the holy gate.

The angels spake : " Presence, that com'st this way,
How wast thou called?"   The shade replied, "*Desaix.*"

" Welcome, great hero from the battle's din,
Reap thy reward forever, enter in."

And, speaking thus, upon his brow they placed
A laurel crown, which ne'er was better graced.

Then, with their flashing glaives of ardent flame
They carved upon the wall his hero-name !

But few of those in history's pages known
Can claim this glorious Eden as their own !

III.

The years went by.   War reveled on the earth,
And the sweet spot of heroes knew no dearth.

But few could stand and to the angels say,
With bleeding limbs, "I, too, was like *Desaix.*"

But once a phantom-soldier sadly came
And stood before the burning swords of flame.

He looked with timorous eyes in mortal awe
Upon the threatening obstacles he saw.

Trembling with fear that naught could dissipate,
He craved admittance at the holy gate.

The angels with distrust upon him gazed,
The swords, curled up like serpents, hissed and blazed.

"How wast thou called?"   "My name was *Bernadotte.*"
"Depart thou hence, poor ghost, *we know thee not!*"

1876.

A LOVE SONG.

I see of men the wicked ways,
  Intrepid acolytes of vice.
I see Sin's snake its venom raise
  And with soft sibilance entice,
While intuition tells my heart
God in all this can have no part.

I see ubiquitous red Crime
  Smile luridly on Peace and Trust ;
I see sweet Candor soiled in slime,
  And Purity befouled by lust !
Falsehood within, Error without,
And God's omnipotence I doubt.

I see blind Justice slyly wink,
  And Truth on altar-steps defiled.
I hear the great minds, formed to think,
  Chatter inanely, like a child.
I see the world in treachery wrought,
And in a higher Power find naught.

I see the pure and guileless doomed
    To daily pain, to hurtful woes ;
I see vast intellect entombed
    By fate that more infernal grows ;
I see all this and humbly cry,
Where is the guarding God on high ?

I see a sceptered maniac lead,
    Like brutes, a host of souls to fight ;
I see brave hearts with anguish bleed
    And rot on gory fields of blight ;
I see Death's scythe on every hand,
And God's *grace* can not understand.

Fire, plague and famine everywhere
    The universal race alarm.
The dooming tempest haunts the air ;
    On earth all banes and venoms swarm ;
I see the ravages of pest,
And can not call Jehovah blest !

Doubt fills me with its cruel bane,
    Tempered by no fallacious lore.
No Bible can avert my pain,
    No Koran to my soul can soar ;

I simply wonder, doubt and say:
Why should God harm us in such way?

But, when I see, in charmed surprise,
  Thy beauty, lovelier than the sea
All haloed by Ionian skies,
  Filled with delight and mystery,
I murmur in my inner soul:
Who gave thee of my life control?

What power occult, benign and rare,
  Gave to thine eyes seraphic light?
What marvel crowned thee with thy hair,
  A grace and glory to the sight?
What force could dower thy perfect lips
To change my spirit's sad eclipse?

I do not know; but when I gaze
  Upon thee, lowly and most meek,
Struggling for words of love and praise
  Too wildly passionate to speak,
A *something* sways me by its rod,
And I at last believe in God.

1881.

GAETANO DONIZETTI.

A thousand godsent melodies found birth,
    And, flower-like, sprang from thine angelic mind,
    To lull the unceasing sorrow of mankind,
And charm the changeless *ennui* of the earth.

Then, when the soul was moved, thy reaper, Mirth,
    Usurped dark Melancholy's throne, and twined
    Light sheaves of song, as buoyant as the wind,
Turning the dross of care to golden worth !

Thy deathless Fame before no tomb shall bow !
    No grave can close upon thy matchless art !
    Cherished, supreme in palace as in mart,
In proud, immortal calm thou standest now,
    With all the grace of Italy in thy heart,
With all the glory of Song upon thy brow !

SUPERIOR.

Since Time began, the sun has wooed with fire
 Vast, virgin solitudes of polar snows ;
And on each marvelous, icy Kremlin throws
 The scintillant rays of its supreme desire.

A thought responsive it may ne'er inspire ;
 The gaunt bergs move not from their bleak repose ;
But, with pure, lingering loves that never tire,
 It offers still one grand auroral rose.

Patient and pleading, ever thrust aside,
 I watch o'er thee, oh ! fair and distant goal ;
 Cruelly conscious of thy utter right,
But nobler far than thy poor, paltry pride,
 I, with the gold auroras of my soul,
 Deluge thy frozen heart with lavish light !

A MOOD OF DON JUAN.

One balmy night, serene with many stars,
　He wandered through the dark lanes of Seville,
　Alone, to young Elvira's domicile,
Deep in the shade of frowning Alcazars.

With no soft pizzicato of guitars
　Or gentle lute, strove he her love to thrill,
　But, sullen, waited, and to suit his will
Her jeweled hand removed the window's bars.

"Is all as I have bidden?" he murmured low.
　"Yea." "And thou lovest me still?" "As worms, impure,
　　Might love some white and wondrous star," she said.
Then in an amorous and morbid throe
　Of mad, crude passion warm lips met secure,
　　Beside a duenna's corpse whose wounds still bled.

1877.

AT THE MORGUE.

Upon the cold, damp slab at rest
  She lies, with her white shoulders bare,
A golden locket on her breast,
  A piece of sea-weed in her hair.

A smile's fair shadow on her lips
  Floats sadly, though those lips are tinged
With purple death, while softly drip
  The sea-drops from her lids, silk-fringed.

Upon a beach of brownish sand
  They found her, on Long Island's shore ;
She held a locket in her hand,
  Upon it was the word " Amor."

The men who found her brought her here
  And on this marble stretched her out,
Where city loiterers come to jeer,
  Where idle throngs parade about.

Is there no one in all this place
 To pray, or murmur a regret
For that sweet-smiling, sorrowed face,
 Half covered by that long hair wet?

Why does she smile, though still and dead?
 Why is her dull stare child-like pure?
See the sweet curving of her head!
 Too fair misfortune to endure.

Yet no one comes — oh! sad, bad earth!
 Has *he* not missed her features mild?
Surely *he* has not spurned her worth;
 She's but a girl, a flower, a child.

See the vast crowds of callous hearts
 Assembling by mere fools' desire
To witness all the morgue imparts
 Of loathsome, horrid, sad or dire.

See them about the cold slabs swarm!
 They gaze on all with mute surprise;
They glance upon her slender form,
 Her smiling lips, her great calm eyes.

They notice on her pulseless breast
  A golden locket — nothing more ;
They leave with murmuring words, oppressed,
  But have not seen the word " Amor,"

Which tells me all the dreadful tale
  Of hopes frustrated, pain, despair —
Which tells me why she is so pale,
  And why that alga decks her hair.

I see, as if in dream, the day
  When she found false the one adored.
  *   *   *   *   *
I see the expectant billows play ;
  I hear how wave and tempest roared.

I see her shuddering face emerge,
  All red with shame and mad with love ;
I see the mists of pearly surge,
  I hear the sea-gull's shriek above !

I see her sink, I hear her sighs,
  Those short, wild sighs, and all is o'er !
Upon her breast a jewel lies,
  A jewel with the word " Amor."

And I can understand it all,
  And that is why I linger here,
To pay a tribute to her pall,
  The simple tribute of a tear.

Upon the cold, damp slab at rest
  She lies with her poor shoulders bare,
A golden locket on her breast,
  A piece of sea-weed in her hair.

THE OLD RAG - PICKER OF PARIS.

When somber midnight glooms the rushing Seine,
  From dismal lanes and famine-haunted slums,
Regardless of the biting sleet or rain,
  The chiffonier with tottering footsteps comes.

Aroused reluctantly from pitying sleep,
  He must begin his long and changeless round,
Pausing before each corner garbage-heap,
  With weary eyes that ever seek the ground.

He sees the glitter of the boulevard,
  The life, the revel and the dazzling glare ;
But from it all his spirit is afar ;
  He totters on without a hope or care.

The merry throngs that rush to ball and *fête*
  Mark not his rags or his dull, searching eye ;
He spurns their silly jests, he can not wait,
  And to his gloom serenely passes by.

He hears no more the drunken roisterer's song,
   The quip and cackle of the noisy crowd ;
The sad, unpeopled streets to *him* belong,
   And, conscious of his sovereignty, is proud.

In barrels foul he thrusts his flickering lamp,
   And in the mass of rubbish, moil and dust,
He sometimes finds, perchance, all soiled and damp,
   A woman's letter, breathing love and trust.

Or scraps of paper, edged with ash and mold,
   His sharp pick stirs before his eyes alert,
Sweet messages in lovers' language told,
   Or poet's rhymes now laureled in the dirt.

But rags and ribbons are alike to him ;
   He can not stop to dream the hours away,
For to his wretched garret, far and dim,
   He must repair before the break of day.

Ah ! strange to think, that in that town, alone,
   This chiffonier, with vacillating feet,
Unheeded, destitute, by men unknown,
   May yet obtain triumphal joys complete !

For a dark day may come when, undismayed,
   He will appear, the favorite of Fame,
And from the height of some red barricade
   Proclaim to earth his everlasting name.

TO AN ANTIQUE MIRROR.

In an old feudal castle hid in France,
   Far in the vine-rich South, I found one day
   A quaint, rare mirror, which all cobwebbed lay,
Its center shattered as if by a lance.

I looked within and saw, like some strange trance,
   The shifting shadows of dead faces play ;
   Pale profiles that have long been dust and clay,
And phantom forms, sad beyond utterance.

And then I dreamed how, in sweet by-gone days,
   The grim queen-mother might have glanced therein
To count her wrinkles and receive no praise ;
   Or how a king, still deaf by Ivry's din,
Might once have held it on his scars to gaze,
   While Gabrielle caressed his tufted chin !

PHOSPHORESCENCE.

With sallow gleams it tints the tranquil waves
　When the wan moon shines holy in the night
On dreaming lakes, or where the Atlantic raves,
　One sees its flickering, sad, phantasmal light.

Proud Science tells us whence it comes and how
　Its force can glimmer in the placid seas.
But, as I watch its trembling beauty now,
　Fancy discovers rarer mysteries !

For when the wonderful and lucent train
　Follows the full-sailed ship that bears me home,
The iron rudder cleaves its mass in vain ;
　A snake of light, it glides amid the foam.

And I, who see this shining marvel pass,
　Feel that the strange glare circling round and round,
Now bright as leaping flame, now dull as glass,
　Must be the imploring eyes of millions drowned !

REVELATION.

Poor, toil-worn student of old Scripture lore,
   Searcher of texts and parables austere,
My youth and love-days dead forevermore,
   What of frail, worldly things had I to fear?

But, ah! the flesh is weak, and mellow June
   Was wild with song of joyous birds, alas!
And, sighing for the fields with roses strewn,
   I looked up from my books and saw you pass.

My weary eyes upon your beauty rare
   Rested in mute and uncontrolled surprise;
My lost youth lurked within your golden hair;
   My vanished dreams were hidden in your eyes.

Pure as the snow, to me your perfect face
   Was like a revelation of the past—
The past that might have been, which, by your grace,
   For one brief spell took life and form at last.

Sweet resurrection, solemn and supreme,
  The lesson of a ruined life to teach !
You were, in possibility, a dream,
  A light that from my gloom I could not reach.

You passed ; and I — well, I stood gazing there,
  And silent wept ; and then returned to plod
Through dreary texts again ; you were so fair
  I had forgotten that there was a God !

PAX ET PURITAS.

Whene'er my sad gaze lingers in thine eyes,
    That glow with all the idyllic warmth of Greece,
    I find from care a lovable release,
My heart throbs faster in a charmed surprise.

Floods of strange fancy wake, and I surmise,
    While subtle pleasures, vaguely known, increase,
    That the calm spirit of delicious Peace,
Candid and beautiful, within them lies.

Then, as I look again, with whims and dreams,
    Another shape appears in stainless white,
      Smiling upon me radiant and fair;
And, to my rapt and ravished mind, it seems
    As if sweet Purity, in robes of light,
      Had come to take eternal refuge there.

1880.

STALACTITE.

The Earth has wept for grievous sins of man,
   For pride of kings and muttered groans of slave.
   It proves no pain in thunders when they rave,
Nor yet in desolate lightnings, blue and wan ;

But mourns, regretful, in some unknown cave,
   Where gleams of sunshine can not reach to scan ;
   Here does it weep, as only Nature can,
Sweet tears, as sweet as violets on a grave.

Deep in its breast, serene, sad breast of woe,
   Deep in its heart, eternal heart of nights,
We find those tears Earth fain would never show
   To all the odium of our torches' lights ;
Those deathless tears, diaphanous of flow,
   Forged in the silence of cold stalactites.

1872.

LANDSCAPE.

The garden, crowned by soft and fragrant June,
   Blooms nonchalant beneath the mute, blue sky.
   In fleecy shoals the stainless clouds pass by ;
Each poplar quivers to a linnet's tune ;

The souls of roses, by the zephyrs strewn,
   Perfume the air in myriads ere they die,
   And seem in redolent agony to lie,
Lacking the benediction of the moon.

An aureole of light tints every tree ;
   Nature, unsullied, dreams her dream of love,
   Wooing the sun unto her nuptial bowers ;
And, in the emerald distance, I can see
   A maiden, white as Aphrodite's dove,
     Pass like a queen amid her sister flowers.

MOTHERS.

Radiant with vernal grace and summer flowers,
    The English landscape in rich splendor glows ;
Half hidden 'mid sweet labyrinths of bowers,
    A snow-white cottage nestles like a rose.

Within a woman sits, supremely blessed.
    Her clear, blue eyes reflect a boundless joy,
When, with long kisses on a loving breast,
    She soothes to sleep her little, dimpled boy !

    *   *   *   *   *

Delhi's majestic temples, domed and porched,
    Tower up in proud, magnificent array ;
The sluggish Ganges, by the fierce sun scorched,
    Gleams like a scimitar in the hot mid-day.

A woman kneels among the reeds and sands,
    Kissing a wee, bronzed child that coos and smiles.
Enough,—great Brâhma speaks !—with trembling hands
    She hurls her first-born to the crocodiles !

EVANGELS.

On earth, for me, there is no woe,
  No burden arduous to bear,
No subtle grief, no hidden foe,
  No dull allurement to despair,
When I, oblivious to all care,
  Turning to calm my saddest sighs,
Can gaze with rapture on the rare,
  The soft evangels of thine eyes.

Fate may retain its direst blow
  For me unblest, and unaware,
May smite me as I dreaming go
  Through life's dark desert, bleak and bare ;
But I hold joy that can compare
  With that of gods, that never dies,
When on me shine divinely fair,
  The soft evangels of thine eyes.

Earth has no bounty to bestow
  That I am ever fain to share ;
Fame, wealth, for me can little show,
  I nothing do, I nothing dare ;
For thee alone my life I spare,
  For thee alone, oh, perfect prize,
Guarding, as heaven would guard a prayer,
  The soft evangels of thine eyes.

ENVOI.

So let my youth be lost, and flow
  Heedlessly by, as wind that flies,
While o'er me with calm rapture glow
  The soft evangels of thine eyes.

THE GALLERY OF THE MIND.

There is a gallery in every mind,
　A mental Louvre full of empty frames ;
　We strive to fill them with desires and aims,
Or try within their void some form to find.

Sometimes a face appears, but half defined,
　Greeting us sadly, and its look proclaims
　A wish fulfilled ; while still another names
That fortune to our secret hopes was kind.

Visions of love and friendship come and go,
　Sad frames, alas ! unfilled, for time remain ;
　　Others, unheeded once, hold faces new,
Welcome in tenderness or sad in woe,
　And so continue through this life of pain,
　　Till death blurs every picture from our view.

IN PÈRE LA CHAISE.

Sweet to my weary soul, the graveyard's glooms
　　Lure me at night their ghostly ways to tread,
And seek among the dismal, moon-bathed tombs
　　The mystic influence of illustrious dead.

The sky, tiaraed with soft starlight, shone
　　On grass-wreathed cippi and old sculptured urns ;
Plaintively sad the lonely cricket's drone
　　Thrilled with weird music the decaying ferns.

Autumn had kissed with sere, pale lips the leaves
　　That cover the dark spot where Musset sleeps,
And the drear wind that for his loss still grieves
　　Caressed his tomb where one bare willow weeps.

Silent, where slumber Davout's valiant bones,
　　I dreamily recalled that life of fame,
Passed 'mid the crash and roar of tottering thrones,
　　Laureled by Auerstadt's and Eckmühl's flame.

Musing of glory still I onward strolled,
    Led by a voice my heart remembered well,
And stood before the tomb of the high-souled
    And peerless child of tragedy, Rachel!

Stupendous Phædra, proud Doña Chimène,
    Before whose art a ravished nation bowed,
Rise from the dust, I cried, and stand again,
    A queen superb, even in thy worm-gnawed shroud.

Poor dreamer, naught could heed my call, alas!
    The fire-flies flittered by me pale and weird,
The night-wind sobbing thro' the wavy grass
    Alone replied, but no sweet ghost appeared.

And then a nightingale in depths near by
    With dolorous strains sang on an humble mound.
Wondering, I sought the name with eager eye,
    And understood when I *Rubini* found.

Lulled by the charms sweet memories invoke,
    Beside this tomb of melody I dreamed,
And when from my enrapturing trance I woke,
    The sun athwart the silent cedars streamed.

PATTE DE VELOURS.

'Twas in a conquered town—we warred in Spain ;
   I was a gay lieutenant, rash and young,
   Loving to lisp the Andalusian tongue
With jet-eyed charmers who to list would deign.

Oft by old Alcazars, with mandolin strung,
   I would not warble long my amorous strain,
And, for my blue eyes' sake, one beauty hung
   Over her balcon's gloom a silken skein.

Deluded boy, with fatuous pride elate,
   I could not deem her love to danger led ;
Yet in that Spanish heart a world of hate
   For me in each soft kiss more surely spread,
And I was found one night beside her gate,
   Her poniard in my throat and left for dead !

FLOWER MAD.

Morbidly languid, through long summer hours
 She lay like some pale rose by dawn dews wet,
 Dreaming amid a mass of mignonette,
Delicious roses and frail Orient flowers.

To cloy her whims insatiable, my powers
 Were taxed before her dainty feet to set
 An Eden of odorous pink and violet—
The sweetest plunder of a hundred bowers.

Ghoul-like she fattened in this flowerful Hell
 That numbed my sense with sickening perfume,
  Until my soul rebelled and would not bow. . . .
She now lies crowned with phlox and asphodel,
 Deep in her chamber's suffocating gloom,
  With one great rose of blood upon her brow!

1877.

BAMBOO.

Whene'er I whirl thee in my fan, I see
   Kaolin turrets and pagodas rise,
   With lanterned kiosks that taper to the skies,
Where languid mandarins sip their perfumed tea.

The gongs of Pekin sound unto the sea,
   The wooden cangue free from a victim lies,
   And in a dream of wonder and surprise
The embattled walls of China tower up free.

Thou canst bring back to me the souvenir
   Of eves when Nankin was begemmed with stars,
     And when Love's summer blossomed in my blood ;
Aye ! when I walked with Tchâ without a fear,
   And kissed in the dim glitter of bazaars
     Her lips as sweet as hawthorn in the bud !

SLEEP'S REGRET.

I, who am called the soother of all ill,
  Who by all mortals am supremely blest,
  Begin by strange misgivings unconfessed
To doubt the power my sweet task to fulfill !

For no nepenthean kiss of mine can still
  The angry fevers of a suffering breast ;
  Soaring Ambition scorns my proffered rest,
And haggard Grief defies my puissant will.

Divinely great, yet sadly incomplete,
  I strive to quell my rage and not despair
    When tortured flesh rebels at my soft breath ;
But all in vain ! I such resistance meet
  That, balked and bitter, I wander otherwhere,
    While grimly beckoning to my brother, Death.

THE IDOL.

STATUE OF VENUS, A. D. 500.

The fickle throngs of Rome no more adore
  My haughty grace in these degenerate days,
  But guard their genuflections and their praise
For one who preached upon a distant shore.

This Christus, whom they worship evermore,
  Could cure all ills, they say, and He could raise
  The buried dead themselves in wondrous ways,
And lull the sullen tempest's fiercest roar.

All this may be, but there will come a time
  When He, the Master who was crucified,
    Will be abjured by all and worshipped never;
While I, in my mute majesty sublime,
  Will still tower o'er them in my marble pride
    And be adored forever and forever!

GRAVES.

The sad night wind, sighing o'er sea and strand,
   Haunts the cold marble where Napoleon sleeps ;
O'er Charlemagne's bones, far in the northern land,
   A vigil through the centuries it keeps ;

O'er Grecian kings its plaintive music sweeps ;
   Proud Philip's grave is by its dark wings fanned,
   And round old Pharaoh's (deep in desert sand
When the grim Sphinx leers at the stars) it creeps.

Yet weary it is of this chill, spectral gloom ;
   For moldering grandeurs it can have no care.
Rich mausoleums in their granite doom
   It fain would leave, and wander on elsewhere,
To cool the violets upon Gautier's tomb,
   And lull the long grass over Baudelaire.

OUTRE TOMBE.

One pale and perfect twilight eve in May,
   Pensive of mood, I sought her cherished tomb ;
   The air was fragrant with a suave perfume,
The earth had woven into flowers the way.

With saddened thought I knelt me down to pray,
   Wondering how Nature, lacking her, could bloom.
   When, oh, most strange ! a rose-bush from the gloom
Caught in my sleeve as if to bid me stay.

I dared not doubt, her fond soul at my feet
   Breathed in the beauteous bosom of the flowers,
And charmed my sense, as when in bliss complete
   Upon the blue Garonne, near feudal towers,
Her white, soft, jeweled hands and kisses sweet
   Were wont to lure me back in vanished hours.

FALSE WORSHIP.

Born in the deep, black hollow of a mine,
    Nursed by weird songs that thrilled my wondering soul.
    I lived amid vast labyrinths of coal,
Taught that, above, God reigned in light divine.

My mother told me, with soft words benign :
    " Of Earth's great mystery thou wilt know the whole,
    The blooming buds and trees will be thy goal,
A paradise of beauty will be thine."

Ah ! sad, prophetic promise ! When she died,
    And, even to my impatient mind, too soon,
        I climbed, in trembling, to the Earth's green sod,
And it was night !   Marveling, unsatisfied,
    I saw the flawless splendor of the moon,
        And swooning, cried in terror, " This is God ! "

VULNERABLE.

When unsymmetric chaos in its might
  Ruled the dim, desolate Earth and left it bare,
  In gloomy caves there wandered everywhere
Amorphous monsters, larvæ of affright.

Deep in the vast, impenetrable night
  They lived and loved, dreading no future care,
  Until their souls were fired by just despair,
When God, to dazzle them, created Light.

Groping like them through life's unhappy gloom,
  I lived in callous stupor, sad and dumb,
    Pleased with my changeless lot without surprise.
Oh! pardoning woman! in thy summer's bloom,
  Why, to illume my dark soul didst thou come
    And blind me with the splendor of thine eyes?

LATIN.

Haunting old volumes of forgotten lore,
   All cultured minds most avidly rehearse
   Its puissant prose, its pure, delicious verse,
Ever unveiling pleasurable store.

Supremely it soundeth as the hollow shore,
   Re-echoing waves, when ired by churchly curse ;
   Noble it is with Cicero and terse,
And sweet on prayerful lips that God implore !

But when I read its lines, unto mine ear
   With grandeur swells the Coliseum's roar !
     I see the stalwart retiarii come
To hurl their grasping nets at glaive and spear !
   And hear her sonorous words choked back by gore
     When life and death hang on a vestal's thumb !

ITALIAN.

Mellifluous daughter of the rigid tongue
   That Rome imperial taught worlds to revere ;
   Like the rich, flawless resonance most clear
Of silver bells are thy soft sounds when sung.

I love thy suave, melodious tones among
   Veronian lanes or Pisan squares to hear ;
   And when in carnival, with jibe and jeer,
Thy words, in air, like fresh concetti are flung !

Before me, when I murmur thee, arise
   Genoa's mart, high palaces and piers,
     Or rosy Capri, redolent with June !
But sweeter still, below calm, starful skies,
   I hear the barcarolles of gondoliers
     In lonely Venice, aureoled by the moon !

ANGLO - SAXON.

High sounding, terse and energetic tongue,
   Like boreal winds, impetuous and rough ;
   There rings in thee the manly, haughty stuff
That suits a brawny chest, a Harald's lung.

Thy harsher beauties by old minstrels sung,
   When tamed to deeper calm, were sweet enough
   To please the robust Saxons, brave and bluff,
Who mouthed thy consonants when thou wast young.

But when thy short, sharp words fall on my ears
   From tutored lips, their rich and powerful sound
     Clangs like steel rapiers smiting brazen shields.
I picture up a revel of hostile spears,
   And hear King Arthur to his foes around
     Trumpet defiant words on battle-fields !

SPANISH.

When with an elegance that deftly strips
   The ancestral Latin of its garb severe,
   How like a rhythmic poem, rich and clear,
Thou soundest on soft Madrileña lips.

To murmur love, sweet as the flower, where sips
   The amorous bee ; in councils, stern, austere,
   But when hate floods the heart, or foes appear,
How thy fierce Moorish gutturals sting like whips !

Language of varied charm, whene'er I hear
   Thy laughing vowels, they invoke the grand
     And babbling turmoil of Granada's mart.
But when thy graver accents strike my ear,
   I see Columbus, praised by Ferdinand,
     Explain with beaming eyes an unknown chart.

GREEK.

Sonorous tongue, thy broad and unctuous speech
   Sounds like soft summer winds through spicy trees,
   Or like the languid plash of idle seas
That kiss the luminous sand on Nauplia's beach.

Fit for a god in prayer, in love to teach
   Warm, amorous hearts serenest mysteries,
   Thy beauty blossomed in Demosthenes,
And placid Plato could thy glories reach.

Yea, even in tame, degenerate Romaic,
   Thy primal grandeur still augustly flows,
And wondrous sounds of melody awake
   Visions of sun-kissed Archipelagoes,
Where hoary Homer, for the future's sake,
   Sang his grand Iliad of sublimest woes.

FRENCH.

Color and grace adorn thy simplest word ;
  Dainty as rhyme thy light, coquettish ease,
  From lips of saucy *gamin* or *marquise*,
Seems like the twitter of some joyous bird.

By all adored, to every tongue preferred,
  Delicate, brilliant, made to flash and please,
  Thy hidden powers and subtle harmonies
By peerless Gautier in his dreams were heard.

But when thy welcome sounds I hear, my mind
  Recalls those gay cafés, where Dumas *père*
    Reveled in wit, puffing his cigarette.
Or, by bold fantasy, myself I find
  Once more a student, on a garret stair,
    Chattering inanely with some pert grisètte.

BETRAYED.

I worshiped her in such devout, strong wise,
  That all the essence of my soul and brain
Dwelt in the vestal violet of her eyes,
  Calm as the ghost-glance of some dead Elaine.

I knew that I alone this gem possessed,
  Remembering years of supplication, ere
I dared to touch the Mecca of her breast,
  Or kiss the tawny Orient of her hair.

I trusted in the smile her pure face wore ;
  I murmured the sweet gospel of her words ;
And would have doubted of her love no more
  Than Summer would have doubted of its birds.

Until, as blind beatitude increased,
  Truth's dismal skeleton, with subtle art,
Sitting beside me at soft passion's feast,
  Showed me that rank, black infamy—her heart.

Ah, God! no hells have torment to compare
  With the mad nameless pain I suffered then—
That mental crucifixion of despair
  Must be alike to Adam's anguish, when,

For the first time, he saw in Eden's bloom
  The luminous day he thought was ever bright,
Swoon by slow changes to the twilight's gloom,
  And die in the black voids of boundless night.

THE SCULPTOR.

TO ROBERT CUSHING.

Life springs from Death inert, at your command,
  A rugged mass is fashioned into grace,
  And the dumb spirit in the marble face
Is beckoned earthward by your magic hand.

Heroes and warriors of our native land
    Live in the Paros Time can not erase,
    And in your studio, like a sainted place.
The hosts of marble dream, serene or grand.

The silent sons and daughters of your brain
      Honor the halls of many a home of arts,
      Or on broad thoroughfares in pride arise.
But when you pass them by in sun or rain,
      You do not hear the throbbing of their hearts,
      Nor see the grateful glory in their eyes !

February, 1887.

THE DROWSY GLADE.

The drowsy glade, all mellowed by the moon,
  Lavished its fragrance through the midnight air ;
The breeze was suave and languorous with June,
  Nature and I waited thy coming there !

I watched the crimson of the roses, strewn
  As if to carpet thee love's pathway rare,
And listened to thy signal, that soft tune
  Once lulled within the great heart of Schubert !

I heard thy footfall ; — joy hath one surprise
  Death can not conquer with its cruel power.
The starry scraps of Heaven within thine eyes
  Still light my soul in that delicious hour
When I in rapture, trusting in thy sighs,
  Culled love upon thy sweet lips like a flower.

TO A MUMMY.

Circled with perfumed bands and sweet with spice,
   Thou lingerest in the stupor of the tomb,
   Beneath great Cheops' everlasting gloom,
With money in thy withered hand, and rice

Wherewith to guard thy spirit from the vice
   Of famished demons, harbingers of doom ;
   And on thy shriveled front still dwells the bloom
Of antique Egypt's palmy Paradise.

Ages have gone, and thou still hast a form,
   While Earth is filled with unarisen dead ;
   Death heaps no horror on thy tranquil head.
Thy limbs are sweet, and night hath kept them warm,
   And the dull eyes, perchance, beneath those lids,
   Have seen the mighty birth of Pyramids !

PENSÉE NOIRE.

The ivy may despise the oak it clings to,
    The bird may hate its song,
Or yet may loathe the peerless star it sings to
    The warm night long.

The rose may sicken of its odor fragrant,
    The bee may hate the rose,
And the stern elms may hate the zephyr vagrant
    That softly blows.

Should it be true that they of such gifts weary,
    Or view them with disdain,
How they must strive in methods vain and dreary
    To end such pain.

But they are doomed reluctantly to cherish
    God's curses and be dumb,
Until the happy hour when they may perish
    Shall slowly come.

If they conceal their suffering, calm and cheerless,
    Before men's searching eyes,
I, from their brave example, must be tearless,
    And hush my sighs.

For I have one most precious consolation
    Which they can never know,
The knowledge of a self-wrought compensation
    While here below.

I scorn the stupid sphere that I was born in,
    God alone knows for what,
And tho' for me it was but made to mourn in,
    I leave it not.

But rather through my coming life of sadness
    I will live on, elate,
Knowing that I, by my fictitious gladness,
    Can make men hate.

1877.

SUFFERING.

Filled with a scorn of life that each day grows,
    Struggling in vain beneath the cruel weight
Of ceaseless and accumulated woes,
    I cursed my sad, inexorable fate.

And, in the haughtiness of wounded pride,
    When Love was dead, when Hope's white doves [had
From the dark depths of my despair I cried,   [flown,
    " The world like mine no suffering has known ! "

But, as I spake, I felt strange languors creep
    Upon me subtly ; my defiant eyes
Were closed in mystic ways, and in weird sleep,
    Dreamful and wonderful, I saw arise

Vague phantoms of the dim, historic past,
    Long-buried dead, whose ghosts now wandered free,
And as I watched them shuddering, mute, aghast,
    Each took a mortal form and gazed on me.

Some among ravenous lions prayed or cowered,
  Gaunt, famished jaws were stained with gory foam,
While in the shadowy distance grandly towered
  The pagan splendor of Imperial Rome!

All vanished ; and through dismal air I saw
  A blade descend, swift, lightning-like and keen,
While specter-mobs, deaf to all love or law,
  Stood, spattered by the blue blood of a Queen !

Then rose a palace girt by Pyramids,
  A marvel of marble, and I heard the gasp
Of one sweet, pearl-crowned woman whose dim lids
  Veiled from her eyes a lithe and angry asp.

This passed, and fettered in a brig's foul hold,
  Strong men lay crowded, dying, while the waves
Were grey with following sharks, colossal, bold,
  Gorged with the vapid flesh of rotting slaves.

Then two sad souls in gardens of delight
  Stood mute and trembling, Sin's supreme reward,
While, pointing outward to disastrous night,
  A pale, stern Angel waved a flaming sword.

All changed again, unnumbered bodies dead,
   Polluting phantom towns from East to West,
Lay stark ; and on their faces in my dread
   I saw the green, warm, gangrenous kiss of Pest.

Then I beheld a turbulent ocean rise ;
   Black, cruel waves rocked corpses tied to spars,
While drowning hundreds with imploring eyes
   Stretched forth wild hands to calm, unpitying stars.

While India's flowerful, fair magnificence
   Before me like a luminous mirage fled,
There, in dire throes of agony intense,
   Gaunt millions cried to Brahma, "Give us bread."

Then, oh, wild dream ! on Calvary I saw,
   By the fierce glare of lightnings wan and white,
With eyes dilated in supremest awe,
   Three burdened crosses in the moaning night.

Mad choruses of unattained desires,
   Hopelessly sad, fell shrill upon my ears.
My sight grew dim by countless flesh-fed pyres !
   I could not span the oceans of dead tears !

Back ! back ! I cried, pale martyrs of the past,
  I did not summon you from endless gloom.
Let not your hates fall on me in their vast
  Completeness, from the portals of the tomb.

Then He, who could in such strange ways invoke
  These tortured spirits and their mad despairs,
Murmured unto me, as I trembling woke,
  " What are *thy* puny sufferings to theirs ? "

DEFRAUDED.

Serenely sailing on far, treacherous seas,
  I slumbered, dreaming of my mother's smiles,
While, gently urged by the Sumatran breeze,
  We passed green groups of indolent palmy isles.

I heard the hissing horror of the storm,
  That spent its fury on our helpless barque,
And through the enormous night I saw a form
  Of leering lightning shoot! then all was dark.

Dazzled and stunned, to sure destruction hurled,
  I woke amid white billows, maimed, alone,
Lost in a foamy hell, a watery world,
  The tortured buffet of the mad cyclone.

For dismal hours one paltry spar and frail
  Gave respite to my hand and grating breath.
I felt the fiber of each muscle fail,
  In clamorous darkness I awaited death.

But as I felt its icy fingers creep
  Upon me, tossed there like some worthless chaff,
No pang of terror made me pray or weep,
  But the grand tempest heard my grander laugh !

For I, about to die in shrouds of foam,
  Whose body in blue voids would leave no path,
Thought of the churchyard worms in my far home,
  And how, defrauded, they would writhe in wrath !

1878.

UNASKED.

Death, swift and pitiless, forever roams
  Around the world with his cortege of woes,
The desecrator of unnumbered homes,
  Patient, terrific and without repose.

Ever before us doth his dusk shade pass,
  The murky churchyards at his bidding thrive ;
There are no chosen, no exempt, alas !
  And he is wretchedest who can survive.

But direr far than Death is one mad thought,
  That grief invokes upon the mourning night,
A thought detested, harrowing, unsought,
  Filling the soul with desolate affright.

Cruel it comes when, worn and overtasked,
  By some dead loss we moan the hours away,
The dolorous thought of questions left unasked
  Before the coffin claimed the lifeless clay.

Too late it is, oh, God, unjust and drear,
  To light the darkness of Death's deep eclipse,
Too late in humble ravishment to hear
  The balm of pardon from those hueless lips.

Why in the days of passion and desire,
  Ere the grim shadow of the tomb drew near,
Did I not whisper all my spirit's fire
  Again, again into her listening ear?

Now the dark sod lies heavy on her head,
  The worm pollutes the roses of her face,
But, ah! the passionate words were never said,
  Unasked, alas! was the ungiven embrace.

Forever and forever are they lost,
  And in no future Paradise will I,
An unbeliever by Doubt's tempest tossed,
  Hear the consoling tones for which I sigh.

Ah, God! from my incredulous, sad heart
  Efface the doubt that ever makes me grieve;
Restore my shattered faith ere I depart,
  Give me the power, the rapture—*to believe*.

1879.

AWE.

A sumptuous board, fragrant with dainty food,
   Awaited me one memorable night,
Where the dear friend I loved, in joyous mood,
   Had bade me haste, to pass in love's delight
      The last of grim December's icy hours
      With luscious wines and women fair as flowers.

Ah! well I now recall our merry jests,
   The trill of laughing beauty, and the glow
Of youth and grace on white Saffonian breasts,
   That screened the bounding love-fed blood below.
      I see again the pulsing marble rise,
      Sweet visions haunt me of ecstatic eyes.

I still can hear the adagio from afar,
   Thro' curtained rooms that reached our ravished ears,
Where Weber's spirit trembled like a star
   Upon a reed, moaning its hopes and fears,
      In such persuasive ways that for a while,
      Moved by its magic, we forgot to smile.

I hear the unsought wit and fancy again
　That flashed in gay caprice from one and all ;
I hear the ripple of the gold champagne,
　The soft lascivious rustle of a shawl,
　　While wanton pleasure on enraptured lips
　　Electrically thrilled white finger-tips.

The perfumed poem of each siren's hair
　Was rhymed with roses by the night-dew wet ;
The pungent redolence of their petals rare
　My retrospective thought can not forget.
　　No soothing drug can from my mind efface
　　This dazzling bacchanal of love and grace.

Flushed by the fiery vintages of France,
　My friend, while murmuring Gounod to his love,
I know not how—he seemed as in a trance—
　Cast his great soulful love-lit eyes above
　　And cried aloud : " Oh, God ! record my vow,
　　That I will love till death as I love now."

Then laughing at the innocent conceit,
　And holding for new wine his fragile glass,
He sneered that God, to make the vow complete,
　Should show His august presence ! but, alas !

The Bible tells us in its solemn grace
No man has lived who once has seen His face !

Made merry by approving smiles, he cried :—
"I doubt this marvelous Being who never shows
His power in splendid and omnipotent pride,
And whose grave features no poor mortal knows.
As false as was my vow, I scorn, dear friends,
This vague, illusive God whose reign ne'er ends."

I, trembling, gazed upon him as he spoke
Defiantly and with a cynic leer.
"Take no more wine," I cried, "for friendship's sake."
He answered not,—a sense of harrowing fear
Came o'er me ; in his dull, fixed eyes, I saw
A look of wild, unutterable awe !

Pallid and mute, with an unearthly stare,
With hands upheld in agonizing dread,
He seemed to groan an incoherent prayer,
And, shuddering, fell upon his face, struck dead.
Then upon all there fell a wondrous gloom,
Something had passed and lingered in the room !

THE MONK.

Ribeira ! when in strange and somber dreams,
　　Haunted by gloomy thoughts I think of thee,
Memory, o'erflowing with thy dismal themes,
　　Pictures sad scenes and bizarre sights to me.

*　　*　　*　　*　　*

I see the sullen moon shine sere and dull
　　Athwart a narrow cloister-chamber bare ;
A wax-light fastened in a human skull
　　Spits in a niche and burns with ghastly glare.

Strange parchments on the humid ground are spread,
　　In one dark corner lies a heap of straw ;
Near it a water-jar, foul crusts of bread,
　　Speaking of penitence and ascetic awe.

Ghost-like in gloom, an antique crucifix
　　Is nailed upon the dark and fissured wall,
The dripping moisture the pale ivory licks,
　　A deadly solitude pervadeth all.

Ah ! sad is he, who mortal hours must pass
　In this foul place, and great must be his worth.
What suffering, prayer and abstinence, alas !
　Until his days are stricken from the earth !

Some holy friar perchance, who, firm, untired,
　Strong in his faith, dwells here and waits the end,
Seeking all-holy truths, by God inspired,
　In Coptic tomes or hieratic Zend.

This austere spot must be the outer shell
　Of his more secret and forlorn retreat ;
Yon dwarf-door leads to some still fouler cell,
　Some loathsome pit of wretchedness complete.

*　　*　　*　　*　　*

I gaze within and find a radiant room,
　Hung with rich tapestries and paintings rare,
In silver vases blushing roses bloom,
　Marble ! gold ! jewels ! glitter everywhere !

A marvel of art, of elegance and grace,
　I see rare wines and fruit in luscious heaps,
While, on a queen-like couch of silk and lace,
　A pale and peerless woman calmly sleeps.

And by her side, kissing a rosary's beads,
    With grave attention and with studious zest,
A young and handsome monk demurely reads
    A well-thumbed Bible on her pulsing breast.

GHOSTS.

In wondrous dreams I saw each separate tomb
  Our world contains, and o'er them in vague swarms
Silently hovered, in unfathomed gloom,
  A multitude of sad phantasmal forms.

I watched their grave and hopeless, searching eyes
  Like vacillant lights that glimmer thro' a mist,
And heard the rush of shadows thro' dull skies
  Holding, perchance, in Death some awful tryst.

Among old tombs they winged a silent way,
  Calling in plaintive tones for souls once dear,
And near untenanted coffins paused to pray
  For one brief spell, then faded back in fear.

Some vainly sought in desecrated ground
  The spot where skeletons, once theirs, might be,
While others wept, they who had never found
  Their white bones hidden by the sorrowing sea.

With lamentable utterance of despair,
    Martyrs that sought a tombstone, in dismay
Learned that their ashes, scattered anywhere,
    Were not inurned by the auto-da-fé.

Some gazed with anguish on the churchyard bare,
    Beholding humble stones, with moistened lids,
While some rejoiced where towered into the air
    The massive splendor of the pyramids.

There, by a dull and sullen moon, I saw
    Draped in imperial robes, with retinue,
A pale, crowned specter, looking down in awe
    Upon the crowded mounds of Waterloo.

It vanished, and a laureled vision came,
    With trembling tread and solemn, tearful eyes,
Murmuring in softest Tuscan one sweet name
    Above the fern-wreathed tomb where Laura lies.

Amid the grim cortege I saw, divine
    As Satan ere the fall, a spirit rare,
Superb and beautiful, yet saturnine,
    Sneer at the empty grave of Baudelaire.

All who upon this sphere had ever died,
  Popes, princes, prelates, warriors, sages, slaves,
Passed in the gloom, some calm or terrified,
  Seeking with eager eyes their dismal graves.

And then, oh, horrid prescience ! I perceived
  My own poor ghost stand lingering above
A desolate tomb, and knew in dreams bereaved
  That it was hers whom I, now living, love !

1877.

PUELLA EROTICA.

She stands most insolent in her gems and gold,
          Haughtily cold ;
Draining the cool Falernian's amber foam ;
     Her palace is the world and she its queen
          Entrancing the obscene
Libidinous patricians of old Rome.

The drunken nobles, gorged with regal feasts,
          Crouch like tame beasts
Before her sandaled feet, and deck with flowers
     The glowing Paros of her perfect breast,
          Pledging with feverish zest
Her stately beauty through the riotous hours.

Effeminate Cæsars, with a Satyr leer,
          Sigh to her ear
Their brutal whims and maddening desires ;
     No gleam of pleasure lingers in her glance
          Fixed on the wanton dance,
Timed by the torment of a hundred lyres.

The boisterous laugh of Rome degenerate
        And passionate
  Breaks thro' the golden hall, but no rare smile
    The indolent coral of her lip illumes ;
        She breathes the heady fumes,
And, statuesque, stands placid in her guile.

Nude slaves drag hampers of rich food and spice,
        Perfumes and ice,
  Unto the reeking, gold-crushed board in haste,
    With monster lampreys from Pompeii caught fresh,
        Fed upon human flesh,
To tempt her morbid delicacy of taste.

The Roman youths have vainly striven for weeks
        Unto her cheeks
  To bring the rose ; and to her lips the strain
    Of joyous song, but all their wealth and power,
        Lavished within an hour,
Move not her proud, indifferent disdain.

Rome is not Rome ! The pampered beauty seems
        To live in dreams,
Shunning of late the gladiatorial fights,

And the mad bacchanals she once adored
Fail, and have not restored
Her shattered mien, nor tendered new delights.

They do not know how the proud beauty burns
With love, and yearns
For one fair, golden-headed galley slave,
Doomed by the Emperor on the coming day
To be the tiger's prey,
And whom by prayer or plea she can not save !

INVOCATION.

My soul regrets the candor that was Rome's,
   When vice was regal, robed in many flowers,
   And when love lingered for long festal hours
Beneath the glory of a hundred domes,
   When in young blood defiant whims grew warm,
   When mighty nations dreamed of perfect form.

Give back, oh, pompous Past, those flawless days,
   And with thy inviolable touch of flame,
   Consume and doom to everlasting shame
The odious present that no mind may praise.
   Oh ! for one hour, in grandeur, here restored
   The stately Pagan past we have adored.

Give back the fountains in thy marble courts,
   Thy perfume-reeking feasts, the witty mart,
   Thy love, thy passion, thy stupendous art,

The carnage of thy gladiatorial sports,
  Send unto us from centuries supreme
  One vivifying glow, one radiant gleam !

Let us once more in marvelous manner see
  Thy triumphs aureoled by Etruscan stars,
  Thy vestal shrines, thy rosy lupanars ;
Oh, slaves of Love, by Art made grandly free,
  Bring back from thy unique, immortal tomb
  One shadow of thy glory in its bloom.

Make the sad apathy within us fresh,
  And deluge it with vital, virile might.
Let potent amplitudes of love and light
Illume the common pulsing of our flesh,
  And pity us, sweet Past, for we are fain
  To learn the lessons thou hast taught again.

Spare us this life in tasteless raiment clad,
  This wreck of color as the world grows old.
Give us again the Sin that Love made glad,
  Give us once more the clang of sound and gold,
And, in the eventless record of our times
Give us the pride and conscience of our crimes.

Bereft of hope, we linger here and burn
    To find again what to thy charm belongs ;
    We need the dulcet clamor of thy songs ;
For some Caligula we madly yearn,
    One who consumes us with his blighting breath,
    But gives us Pleasure if he gives us Death.

1878.

POSTHUMOUS REVENGE.

The one I loathed, my one malignant foe,
  He who had marred my life in cruel wise,
Lay mute before me, nevermore to rise,
  Pierced to his treacherous heart by one quick blow.

With hate ineffable, with withering scorn,
  I guarded there his carrion, dark and dead,
And, till the misty advent of the morn,
  Gazed in his dull, unanswering eyes of lead.

But not content, with rage that nothing daunts,
  I hissed into his ear my joy of crime,
With haughty insults, with infernal taunts
  And all that hideous hate could make sublime.

And then, oh, God! while I stood fearless there,
  Alone in that deserted, sullied place,
I heard, I heard, a murmur of despair,
  A hot, swift *something* struck me on the face!

Pallid with anger, I did quickly turn,
  To cruelly chastise the foe unknown.
I felt the warm wound on my forehead burn,
  But, oh ! avenging God ! *we were alone !*

Then horror held me, while I no thing saw,
  I sank unto my knees without control,
For I had understood at last, in awe,
  That what had struck me was his *outraged soul !*

1880.

CAPRICES OF DEATH.

Filled with a stern, unutterable pride,
  He counts the remnant of each mortal's hours,
And moves implacable on every side,
  Strong in the knowledge of unquestioned powers.

For him no time exists, no day, no night,
  Despotic law within him sterner grows,
And his dull eyes, with infamous delight,
  Watch mighty universes decompose.

White Hope lies dead upon his threshold's gloom,
  Of moaning mercy he has had no care;
Ordained to fill one never-closing tomb,
  Slave of an angry God, he can not spare.

But, though his fatal shafts must surely fall,
  With all the terror of their cruel weight,
On bird, on man, on blossom, crushing all,
  The good, the vicious, the obscure, the great,

He can, to please a ghastly mood, postpone
  The livid horrors of the final throes,
And can protract the dying sufferer's groan,
  Or numb the toad that desecrates the rose.

In slaughterous war his cruel spirit tires
  To see strong men succumb with trifling pain,
Deep in the Inferno of the cannon's fires
  Or in the deluge of the bullets' rain.

He fain would force the hosts he dooms to die,
  By haggard famine and mad thirst oppressed,
To suffer more, and wearies of the cry
  Of thousands rotting in some purple pest !

He loves to spread the gnawing cancer's seed,
  That slowly blossoms into grim decay,
And cause again some half-healed wound to bleed,
  Or bid the worm consumption eat its way.

Ever creating pain and torture new,
  He roams among us, and has heard me cry
With feverous faith that nothing could subdue :
  "Death, thou hast spared me ! Yet I wished to die."

And now he leers at me in direst way,
　As, fearless, I await his laggard call,
But, oh, the agony of this long delay !
　What *can* he seek, *my* spirit to appall ?

1877.

DEVIOUS PATHS.

Friend, fate ordains we part no more to meet,
  No ray of hope can our hearts' gloom dispel ;
No future will unite us, far and sweet,
  For life and death we now must say farewell !

You go where Cuba, draped in flower and palm—
  The blonde Sultana of the Antilles—
Dreams to the languid sun in tropic calm,
  Girt by the sapphire of voluptuous seas.

While I, whose whole soul thirsts for bird and bloom,
  On whom dire fortune no kind gift bestows,
Must dwell for ever in the boreal gloom
  Of grim Archangel's sun-defying snows.

The dreamy southern breezes to your ear
  Will waft delicious and melodious strains ;
While I in dismal solitudes will hear
  The gaunt wolf's dolorous howl on sleety plains.

Ah ! friend, I envy you.   Strange thoughts of dread
    Follow and fill me with persistent power ;
I feel that I shall rest when I am dead
    Where ice-winds moan and awful glaciers tower,

While o'er the tomb where you will mutely lie
    Luxuriant trees will pitying foliage wave,
Bright, anxious stars will guard you in the sky,
    And hosts of roses will caress your grave.

Ah ! then, when freed by death, sweet spirit divine,
    Though you be shadow, mirage, fire or form,
Fly through chill space to seek the soul once mine,
    And clasp and cling to me till I am warm !

WAVE TO WAVE.

Roll on, my fearless one, the storm advances ;
  Roll shoreward, oh, my mighty lover wave,
And o'er the ocean's turbulent expanses
  Rush with impetuous fury, grand and brave !

Calmly will I await thee, deep leagues under,
  And all my soul will guide thee, when the shock
Of thy tremendous avalanche, like thunder,
  Falls with a roar upon the haughty rock !

Be not like young lake billows, idle dreamers,
  Cowards that bitter Boreas fails to vex ;
Roll on resistless, tear and rend huge steamers,
  Cover our seething domain with their wrecks.

Scourge with a whip of foam, oh ! love victorious,
  The feeble ships that dare to brave thy might,
And hiss the songs I love when, strong and glorious,
  Thy pliant arms assail the beacon's light

And, oh! my faultless hero, sternly reckless,
　Rise up and strive to grasp the hateful stars,
And bring to me for bridal gift a necklace
　Of shells and dripping alga, bones and spars.

How beautiful thy form must seem when lightning
　Illumes the tangled vortex of thy hair!
And when the moon, thy sinuous graces heightening,
　Looks fondly on thee from the silent air!

And, oh! sweet wave, when praises thou art earning,
　Remember that my heart will constant keep,
And with strong faith to thy love ever turning,
　I will await thee in the awful deep.

THE CROSS SPEAKS.

For years in towering stateliness I stood,
The lord of cedars, in the holiest wood
  That bloomed upon the hills of Lebanon ;
Guarding the purity of many a nest
With softly swaying boughs, and ever blest
  By gentle rains and by the soothing sun.

Below me roamed the solemn, peace-eyed herds
That craved my shade, and, glorified by birds,
  In tranquil ways I breathed sweet life away ;
While the consoling, clover-scented breeze,
Wafted in perfume from the Grecian seas,
  Caressed me at the sultry close of day.

My life was one of sanctity and balm,
And nothing marred the monotone of calm
  Haunting the ample woodlands where I dreamed.
My base was sprent with miracles of flowers,
And in the distance I could see the towers
  And spires of Sidon when the sunlight gleamed.

But on one eve, strange men, with shining blades,
Passed like a boisterous tempest thro' the glades,
　　And paused before my beauty fair and tall,
And one, rough-voiced, with large, admiring eyes,
Counting my branches that assailed the skies,
　　Cried, "Seek no further, this good tree must fall!"

Then to the core they struck me with sharp steel;
I felt the sap within my veins congeal,
　　I writhed and moaned at every savage blow,
And I, whose strength had braved the fiercest storm,
Tottered and fell, a mutilated form,
　　While all the forest waved its leaves in woe!

Then fashioning from my boughs, with rough, swift hands,
A cross colossal, girt with iron bands,
　　They dragged me in my pitiful disgrace
Down to the holy town Jerusalem,
There to give death to those the laws condemn,
　　And placed me in a sad, accursèd place.

Defiled, I stood there, mourning for my leaves,
While on my breast they nailed the city's thieves,
　　With livid martyrs and assassins grim,

Who rent the air with horrid cries of pain,
Lingering upon me, calling death in vain,
   Crow-gnawed and shivering in each tortured limb.

Severe and constant were the dread decrees
Of Pontius Pilate, and the agonies
   Of countless victims granted me no rest ;
My wood was soiled by blood and split by nails ;
I lived in one mad hell of harrowing wails ;
   By carrion weights I ever was oppressed !

Then came a dark and sacrilegious day
Of crime, of malediction, of dismay !
   Rude soldiers tore me from the hated ground,
And brought me, with foul oaths and many a jeer,
Before one pale, sweet Man, who, without fear,
   Did tower above them, godlike, nettle-crowned !

Shrill voices, formed to curse and to abuse,
Cried, choked with scorn, " Ignoble King of Jews !
   Save thyself now if that thou hast the power."
But He, the meek one, resolutely caught
My hideous body to Him and said naught ;
   And God was with us in that awful hour !

Thrilled by His touch, a sense I never knew
Sudden within my callous fibers grew,
   Warning my spirit He was pure and good.
And I could feel that He was Christ divine,
And that a deathless honor then was mine,
   In one dark instant I had understood !

The raucous shouts of thousands rent the air,
When on His outraged shoulders, scourged and bare,
   He bore to dismal Calvary and night
My ponderous weight, my all-unhallowed mass,
While I, God-strengthened, strove and strove, alas !
   Without a hope, to make the burden light.

He perished on my heart and heard the moan
That shuddered thro' me, He, and He alone.
   But no man heard the promise He gave *me*
Of sweetest pardon, nor did any mark
His pitying smile that aureoled the dark
   For me, in that wild hour on Calvary !

When tender women's hands, that sought to save,
Had carried His sweet body to the grave,
   A streak of flame hissed forth from heaven and rent

My trunk with one annihilating blow,
Leaving me prostrate, charred, too vile to know
　　That I was nothing, and God was content.

But He who punished my sad sin with fire
Forsook me not in my abasement dire,
　　And mercifully bade my soul revive,
To take new spells of life, that all might see,
With beauty far exceeding any tree,
　　Once more with resurrected leaves to thrive !

And now, in verdurous calm, adored of birds,
Circled by flowers and by the tranquil herds
　　That love beneath my stateliness to browse,
I dream in peace through hours of sun and gloom,
And near unto the Saviour's worshiped tomb
　　I wave my soft and sympathizing boughs !

RIVALS.

I.—KUNCHIN-JINGA.

Himalayas.

Majestic and sublime in icy splendor,
　I stand alone, vertiginously high !
　My peaks colossal pierce the swooning sky,
And winds unknown to man sweet homage tender,
　As o'er my scintillating heights they fly,
And mystic secrets to my soul surrender !

The stars grow pale at my ascent laborious,
　For heavenward I immaculately climb !
　Wrapped in the dazzling mantle of my rime,
Towards them I rear my threatening crests and glorious,
　While unto earth I hurl, in wrath sublime,
My avalanches ponderous and victorious !

Along my glittering crags the somber thunder
　Bounds at my will, and the intolerant sun
　Pours down to harm me rays I never shun !

In frigid grandeur I discern far under
  The timid clouds that, since Time has begun,
Veil my abysmal base, and pass, and wonder !

Men insolently bold have dared, for glory,
  To scale me, grandest of God's earthly thrones !
  My shifting glaciers echoed with their groans,
When down deep leagues of chasm, inert and gory,
  They fell !—so far, I can not see their bones
On dim plateaux below, that tell the story !

And yet they cried (oh, sad humiliation !)
  That other mountains with my height could vie.
  But I, that am a portion of the sky,
Gaze down in scorn upon their desolation,
  Watching them count their numbered days and die,
Serene in my eternal domination !

For India, in her beauty fair and flowerful,
  Kneels at my feet, and, with a cult intense,
  Adores my august grace, in jungles dense,
On sultry plains and in Benares towerful !
  While in my motionless magnificence
I stand, her luminous guardian, pure and powerful !

For I exist unique in wild space cheerless,
  Crowned by the stars, encompassed by the earth ;
  No eye can span the terror of my girth,
Nor desecrate my summits, proud and peerless ;
  For God hath dwelt within me from my birth,
And I alone have listened to Him, fearless !

II.—CHIMBORAZO.

Andes.

Of mighty storms and blighting winds prolific,
  Lord of a continent, I nobly stand !
  Green leagues of rich and forest-bosomed land
Look in dumb fear upon my steeps terrific,
  And, like cowed slaves, at my foundations grand
Crouch the vast billows of the blue Pacific !

White as a thought of God above, transcendent,
  My lofty cliffs in glacial glory loom !
  A lily of ice, I insolently bloom
In marvelous chastity of frost resplendent ;
  While o'er unfathomable gulfs of gloom
My awful leaves of snow are poised and pendent !

My feet by clouds are ever shrouded densely,
    But far above, in grace without a flaw,
    I surge, and with my luminousness awe
Pale hosts of shivering satellites immensely ;
    And chill by my omnipotence and law
The vague, sad moon that worships me intensely !

The tame world trembles in severest panic
    When gazing on the wonder of my face !
    And when my ire, from pinnacle to base,
Is hurled with maddening force and throes volcanic,
    Vast haughty cities sink and leave no trace,
While I remain serene and diaphanic !

What hill in the hot East to me, a giant,
    Dares to compare its unessential height ?
    I, who before the sullen sun gave light,
Illumed the world and led strange monsters pliant
    To seek my caverns in the woeful night,
When I alone stood arrogant, defiant !

No ! in my pride, erect for countless ages,
    I can disdain of rivalry to dream !
    A thousand tempests, that above me scream,

Have told me, and their voice my wrath assuages,
   That I alone am perfect and supreme,
That I can scorn these Oriental rages !

And tranquilly my mighty spirit ponders,
   Conscious no mountain with my strength can vie,
   For I can make unnumbered nations die,
When through dark, dismal caves my anger wanders,
   And I remain immortal as the sky,
Proud in my awful coronet of condors !

CARLO ALBERTO CAPPA,

Band-Master Seventh Regiment, N. Y. S. M.

No paltry preference of school is thine,
　Thy soul finds room for all called great and true.
　Mozart and Gluck are perfect in thy view,
In thee no stale comparisons combine.

Weber, and Bach, and Donizetti shine ;
　The older styles are treasured with the new.
　Verdi and Händel have from thee their due,
And all who hold the passion-spark divine.

Thy genius finds the jewels of their thought,
　The mystic secrets of their deathless song,
　And all the lessons that to them belong
Unto our willing ears thy wand has taught,
　And in the future, as to-day, thy name,
　Honest, eclectic, will go down to fame.

FLEUR DE RIZ.

When vagrant fancy thy strange charm recalls,
  Ravished, I think of those fair dames who graced,
  With *mouche* on lip, light foot and wasp-like waist,
The stately splendor of the Bourbon balls.

At Versailles, through the vast and frescoed halls,
  I watch them, perfumed, rouged and satin-laced,
  Dance the minuet with that entrancing taste
Which every true and knightly mind enthralls.

And then again, as dream to dream doth pass,
  I see the Regents' *roués*, warm with wine,
    Chat with blonde Sabran or pert Parabère,
And sloe-eyed Manon at her looking-glass,
  Beckoning Des Grieux with an amorous sign,
    To unwind the powdered marvel of her hair !

BLUE BLOOD.

A SANS-CULOTTE SPEAKS. 1793.

I hate her white, aristocratic face,
　The grand and stately manner of her mien !
She steps among us in patrician grace,
　Conscious of birth, as if she were a queen.

She loves alone the antique pedigree
　Her sires by valor through Crusades possessed,
The couchant lion and the *fleur-de-lys*
　That gleam with golden gules upon her crest.

Her pale lips scorned me when, in fearful strife,
　I drew her outraged body from the mud,
Dashed pikes aside and saved her worthless life,
　Yea, spurned me like a hound !　I had *no blood.*

Not *blue*, but scarlet, pure, and yet this proud
　And supercilious hussy, reptile-souled,
When I had driven back the hooting crowd,
　Flung in my gory face a purse of gold !

And I had *touched* her ! oh ! the heinous crime !
　　I, low and vulgar, although brave and kind !
Her blood was taintless and my own of slime,
　　Or little better to *her* feeble mind.

Sick of this paltry pedigree of birth,
　　I to the Assembly have denounced her name,
And no defending sword that shines on earth
　　Can save her haughty carrion from shame.

Chained in a fetid prison dark and bare,
　　She lies with loathsome creatures all unclean,
And her blue blood, thank God and Robespierre !
　　Will wash to-day our dirty guillotine !

TO MAX MARETZEK

*On the occasion of the fiftieth anniversary of Mr. Max Maretzek's ap-
pearance as an impresario and manager.*

Master! thy chosen mission in this land
   Was one of melody and art divine ;
   Thou cam'st to purify and to refine,
And teach us what was beautiful and grand.

Thy restless spirit, nurtured to command,
   Warmed us and moved us like a generous wine ;
   While every honor of this boon is thine,
Created by thy brain and nobly planned.

The deathless bays are many on thy brow ;
   Thou hast not labored o'er life's path in vain ;
At lofty shrines thy head alone would bow.
   Therefore our gratitude can never wane,
And for all time, thy memory, as now,
   Sweet and imperishable will remain.

THE CATACOMBS OF PARIS.

Far through their ghastly corridors I went,
  Bringing to holy glooms my doubting breath,
Seeking to purify my discontent
  By grim communion with such trace of death.

Down, down into the solemn depths and dim,
  Onward, thro' oozing vaults and windings drear,
To please the morbid fever of my whim,
  I wandered resolute and without fear.

Enormous Golgothas of mildewed bones,
  Gaunt, reeking skeletons, corrupt and bare,
Upon the Ossuary's humid stones,
  In awful symmetry lay everywhere !

And in the slimy horror of the sight
  My heart grew warm, while trepidation fled ;
And the vague dawning of a strange delight
  Came o'er me there among the crowded dead.

Within this dismal Campo Santo then
  I strove again the varied past to trace
Of all those mute, sad myriads of men,
  For centuries moldering in their dark disgrace.

The bullet-shattered skull, which I now hold,
  Perchance saw Jena's desolating flame,
And when the ruin of the cannon rolled,
  Defying death, called on Napoleon's name !

And yonder shining, yellow lump of clay,
  On whose grim jaw my lantern's radiance flits,
May have upheld, thro' one terrific day,
  The peerless Emperor's flag at Austerlitz.

That other, severed from its withered trunk,
  Tottered perhaps in bloody mists unseen,
Save by the furious rabble, powder-drunk,
  Howling their hates around the guillotine !

And even those pitiful, decaying rows
  Of senseless skulls that I now gaze upon,
May hold together, side by side—who knows ?—
  The godless debauché, the patient nun !

Oh ! awful minglement ! oh ! dream of fear !
  The bones of lovers may be cast apart,
And the sad victim may be stationed here
  Next to the dead tormentor of his heart !

The hour had come ; I left the dolorous gloom
  To go to light and the abodes of men,
Glad of release, yet knowing that my doom
  Would lure me, lifeless, to its depths again !

QUARTETTO D'ITALIA.

NAPLES:—THE LAZZARONE.

Vesuvius, tranquil on its lava steeps,
    Towers treacherous o'er the bloom of many trees,
    Courting the orange-scented Ischian breeze,
That near its fuming summit faintly sweeps.

Among rich, amber fruits in luscious heaps
    The lazzarone dreams by dreamy seas ;
    Or, on the Chiaja, in delicious ease,
Scorning the fierce sun, indolently sleeps.

But sometimes the grim mountain hurls its fire
    To earth and air with deadly throbs of light,
      As if to tell the world its awful needs !
And, when war warms the lazzarone's ire,
    He also wakens, while the placid night
      Showers star-light on his great, heroic deeds !

THE APPENNINES:—THE BRIGAND.

Behind thick vines he paces to and fro,
 Grasping a carbine strung with ribbons gay ;
 Tiger-like waiting for a chance to slay,
While fires infernal in his dark eyes glow.

The sunny roads no weary traveler show,
 And the dull, idle hours are whiled away
 In dreams of deeds that may surpass some day
The bloody fame of Fra Diavolo !

Then, when is heard a slow, advancing tread,
 Coward unto the heart, he swift will hide
  To send his bullet with supreme address !
And, as he robs his victim, prone and dead,
 In all the ignorance of his surly pride
  He thanks the Virgin for his foul success.

ROME :—LA TRASTEVERINA.

She wanders through the lightless lanes of Rome,
 A flower of grace, with grave, nocturnal eyes ;
 To her belong the calm Italian skies,
And all the Eternal City is her home.

In drugget wrapped she stands, and from her comb
　　Falls the dusk torrent of her hair, that flies
　　Windward, and in the twilight's tint that dies,
Her white teeth glimmer like the fleeting foam.

And I, who by fond words can call her mine,
　　Think, when I hear her sweet and pleading sighs,
　　Of subtle phantoms resurrect at last :
For in the willow of her arms that twine
　　Their softness round me, I can feel arise
　　The Imperial Messalinas of the past !

VENICE:—THE GONDOLIERS.

O'er many a blue and palace-girt lagoon
　　Idly from dawn to twilight thou dost skim,
　　With face patrician, perfect in each limb,
Languidly humming some Bellinian tune.

Or to the Lido, where the roses strewn
　　Please for an hour thy vague, poetic whim,
　　Thou leadest in the night from bridges dim,
Thy donna, white as the attendant moon.

But then again, some quick and avid eye
May watch thee, noiseless, in the shadows lurk,
While all the town is maddened by guitars,
And, as thy heedless rival saunters by,
Can see thy sharp and jewel-hilted dirk
Angrily glint beneath Venetian stars !

A FAREWELL.

TO MARIE B———.

" *Senza te son nulla.*"—PETRARCA.

I must leave thee, for my fate has called me yonder,
　To the future's night of sorrow and of pain ;
With my anguish I must struggle on and wander
　Ere our faces meet in ecstasy again.

Hope as staff for my long roaming I have taken,
　And thy love will ever be my guiding star ;
From my feet the dust of unbelief is shaken,
　And the nothingness of things that were and are.

To new life I start again and have arisen,
　I leave all save thine imperishable part ;
I am free, and yet I linger on in prison,
　In the chaste and wondrous prison of thy heart.

I abandon naught that maketh me regretful,
　For thy love I take as banner and as sign,

And the days will pass and leave me unforgetful
  Of the memory of the kisses that were thine.

If I turn the book of life and find new pages,
  If fame lavishes on me its rarest fruit,
I will tell the wondering multitude of ages
  How attainment in thy spirit found its root.

And with golden words and phrasing as of fire,
  With resistless love and constancy as aim,
I will scale the rock of glory and aspire
  To engrave upon its height thy worshiped name !

I will parry for thy sake fate's sword with boldness,
  Of my passion's warmth no pain can chill the glow,
I will brave the world's derision and its coldness,—
  Do not violets bud and blossom under snow ?

For I love thee like the day, when, sunshine-sated,
  It sinks lingering in the twilight of its swoon,
And I love thee with sweet fervor unabated,
  As some calm lake loves the glimmer of the moon.

In my heart's unwavering faith thy gentle face is
  Ever present in its virginal, sad calm,

Through life's desert thou art ever my oasis,
  And thy beauty is my date-tree and my palm.

Yea! I love thee for the generous love thou givest
  To illume the tortuous by-roads of my gloom ;
For thou lov'st to temper evil as thou livest,
  As the lilies love to lavish their perfume.

Through the bane and blight of malice and of sneering,
  Through the hate-storms that will surely round me
        crowd,
I will see thy glance triumphant in its cheering
  As the beam of some pale moon athwart a cloud.

And the thought of past and future will protect me,
  As the trust thou hast confided unto me ;
And the knowledge of thy virtues will delect me,
  As the scent of honey gratifies the bee.

I will love thee with a love that never falters,
  With a steadfast love that knows not rest or peace,
And the incense I will burn upon thine altars
  Will be pure and sweet as memories of Greece.

For without thy love my spirit lives in peril,
  On my crest of faith pale absence leaves a stain ;
For I need thee as some sun-scorched meadow sterile
  Needs the rare, refreshing ripple of the rain.

And, remember, through my midnights and my morrows
  I shall live, I shall exist but for one thing ;
I shall wait for thee thro' troubles and thro' sorrows,
  As the linnets wait the coming of the spring.

And, remember, should I lose thee, all is ended,
  For without thy love my voice can not be heard,
And thou art as much of me, if souls are blended,
  As a sweet song is a portion of a bird !

Oh ! my sweet one, oh ! thou splendor of my yearning,
  Oh ! thou beauty that my nullity has won ;
To thy love my spirit ever will be turning,
  Like the heliotrope's pale petals to the sun.

I will drug my heart so deeply with hope's lotion,
  That its essence ne'er can dwindle nor will die,
I will imitate hopes hopeless, like the ocean
  When its billows break in foam to see the sky.

For as Poesy thou art gentle and alluring,
  And the love I give the muses of my soul
Will but aid my love for thee to be enduring,
  And will help me as I struggle for my goal.

'Tis for love of thee I live ; I dare not linger,
  When I hold our future happiness at stake,
And the day will come when time's approving finger
  Will do honor to the sacrifice I make.

For if care should dull thy face to me and blind it,
  Through the sadness and the ennui of the years,
I will seek its peerless purity and find it
  In the sympathizing mirrors of thy tears.

And, oh ! darling, if death's sickle cares to number
  All my blooming life-grain breaking free from tare,
Thou shalt feel my spirit hover in thy slumber,
  In the gold and in the perfume of thy hair.

And when I, if dead, some heavenly power am sharing,
  I will watch thee and protect thee from above,
And, still faithful, I will comfort thy despairing,
  And will strive to send thee proof of all my love.

EN SOURDINE.

A MOOD OF MADNESS.

The one I loved would my sad presence spurn,
  When, with a weary heart, I sought the balm
Of Chopin's dreamy, worshipful Nocturne,
  Or Schubert's sighs and Weber's puissant calm.

Soft tearful songs, on trembling pedal low,
  Chilled her dull heart as would dark, icy vaults ;
But happy crimson on her cheek would glow
  When with quick bass I thrummed some noisy waltz.

And when, within my silent studio's gloom,
  My spirit blent with melodies most rare,
Her rich contralto from a distant room
  Would trill in ecstasy some vulgar air.

She maddened me by inartistic greeds ;
  But, for her sake, ah ! sweeter were the rack ;
My feverous fingers, like strong, goaded steeds,
  Rushed through the jingles of an Offenbach.

Until one night when, dreaming in the dark,
    She came to me and craved a senseless song ;
She saw not in mine eyes the deadly spark,
    She could not hear my anger's throb and throng.

I hushed her voice forever with cold steel ;
    I felt my brain in utter frenzy burn * * *
And o'er her corpse inert, with maniac zeal,
    I played sweet Chopin's worshipful Nocturne.

SOUVENIRS.

Return, sweet dream, to soothe my ceaseless pain ;
　I need the winning balm thy coming grants ;
It speaks to me of the glad past again,
　The golden days of youth in sunny France.

When the far future had no vague alarm,
　And when my heart held resolute belief
In purity and love, sweet days of charm,
　Untainted by the bitterness of grief.

I see once more my cozy student room,
　The pipe and foils, the curious old chair,
Wherein, till twilight draped me in its gloom,
　I smiled with Gautier, raved with Baudelaire.

I see myself again, when times were dull,
　Wandering upon the glittering Boulevard,
Writing romantic sonnets to a skull,
　Or dubious songs for some new Alcazar.

Sweet dream, thou cans't revive the happy time,
    When for Art's sake my last old coat was pawned,
To see within the Louvre's walls sublime
    The dazzling, peerless grace of La Joconde !

And when, with absinthe and with cigarettes,
    I vainly strove to give the perfect form
Of towering statues to my statuettes
    And dash off plays like " Marion Delorme."

Alas ! my dream, all is not kind with thee !
    The Morgue's white, trickling slabs thou dost recall,
And, pale upon one, I forever see
    The poor, drowned friend I cherished above all.

And he,—ah ! well. I can not now reprove
    The heartless girl who lured from Art and Fame
His noble soul to Death's eternal groove.
    I pity both ; I might have done the same.

Oh, dream ! bring back no visions such as these,
    But lead me rather to fair Fontainebleau,
Where, with the warmest of warm Burgundies,
    We drank to Dumas ! Hugo ! Géricault !

Echo the merry jests that all day long
   Made life a joy in those ecstatic hours,
When youth trilled, bird-like, its great bliss in song,
   When we existed but for Art and flowers !

And when, in the deep, violet-haunted glade,
   Two dusk-brown eyes of velvet and of flame
Drooped their delicious light, while half-afraid,
   Pure lips first softly murmured "*Oui, je t'aime.*"

Return, sweet dream, too soothe my ceaseless pain,
   I need the winning balm thy coming grants ;
It tells me of the glad, mad past again,
   The golden days of youth in sunny France !

DE ANNA, KING OF BARITONES.

Thou art the Ashton of *Gaetano's mind ;
　　Thou art the real Chevreuse his fancy sought ;
　　Thy heart knows well his heart, thy thought his thought;
His inspiration in thy voice we find.

New laurels for his fame thine art can bind,
　　The value of his genius thou hast taught ;
　　His subtlest meaning thou hast ably wrought,
And in thy soul his memory is enshrined.

With firmest feet thou tread'st the path of fame,
　　Charming all men by thy prodigious art,
　　But still a vast regret o'erfills my heart,
Wherein I hear the praises of thy name,
　　For Donizetti, dead, can not rejoice
　　And marvel at the glory of thy voice!

1886.

*Gaetano Donizetti.

A CAPRICE.

I might have won that love as sweetest prize
  You offered me in passion uncontrolled,
But, like a beggar with averted eyes
  Who passes, heeding not the scattered gold,
I went my way, unconscious of your pain,
Lured by illusive dreams and fancies vain.

You held unto my parched and trembling lips
  A chalice, burning with a hope divine,
But no love's light shone through my soul's eclipse.
  I did not taste the rare, consoling wine.
While thirst-consumed, to arid goals I went,
Filled with the poisons of my discontent.

This was your thought, oh, woman ! you did not know
  How it delighted my imperious pride
To see your maddening loveliness bend low
  And crave my love, ever unsatisfied,
Merely to rob you of your life-long peace,
And please an idle whim, an hour's caprice.

NAPOLEON.

Thy breath was fire ! And fire was on thy brow !
  Dealing out lightnings on thy ceaseless tramp,
Thou mads't the heads of haughty kings to bow,
  When the exultant welcome of thy camp
  Hailed thee in summer's heat and winter's damp.

Born for a day, thou Destiny dids't know,
  And, eager, longedst thy victories to claim !
Thy soul-star shown on Borodino's woe,
  On Jéna's corpse-strewn field, in Wagram's flame !
  Europe, o'erawed, crouched shuddering at thy name.

Hark to that echo born of crushing glooms
  That o'er thy sepulcher continually flits !
It is the murmur of ten thousand tombs !
  Each soldier-corpse stiff in his coffin sits,
  Hailing the thunders of thine Austerlitz !

Dost thou, oh, giant ! lead those warriors still
  In other planets to the valorous strife ?
Dost thou urge on thy phalanxes to kill ?

And art thou doomed to lead a battling life
In other spheres, all gore and combat-rife?

Art thou by God to crush his foes ordained,
	Far on the limits of the endless night?
Art thou still chief, and hast thou battles gained
	With countless myriad angels in the fight?
	Hast thou *His* sword of flame to sheathe or smite?

If so, oh! do not grieve for our sad earth,
	The men that loved thee are no longer true;
They have forgotten all thy priceless worth;
	Long are thy deeds lost as the years grow new,
	All that they know of thee is —— Waterloo!

1873.

GRETCHEN.

From the Italian of Lorenzo Stecchetti.

Near the Cathedral door, as black and base
  As some foul witch loved by a demon crew,
  Squatting in filth, a weird hag met my view,
The mark of bagnios stamped upon her face.

But in the Beldame's wrinkles I could trace
  A vestige of dead beauty glimmering through ;
  Therefore, I asked, "What somber Fates pursue
Thy life and make thee peddle in this place?"

She answered : "*I was Marguerite!* For gold
  I have unnumbered men since Faust enticed,
    And given to each my gladdened kiss of sin.
And now, to warm my withered flesh so old,
  I sell these images of Saints and Christ
    To buy myself a penny's worth of gin."

THE KISS.

Incorrigible, false coquette,
  She spurned my love and with a smile
Bade me her promises forget ;
  Toying with glittering rings the while.
    (But tell it not.)

Doubting of old her inconstant heart,
  The dreaded blow was less severe ;
Wicked, she turned to see me start,
  Or mark, perchance, a falling tear.
    (But tell it not.)

"If it must be, if cherished bliss
  Is lost to me forever," I cried,
"Give me one last, sweet, parting kiss,
  To soothe my passion's injured pride."
    (But tell it not.)

With pretty gestures, like a bird
  In her rare loveliness unique,
She, smiling, rose, without a word,

And gently kissed my lips and cheek.
    (But tell it not.)

*   *   *   *   *   *   *

That peerless beauty, chaste and proud,
    Lies in her sumptuous coffin now !
Her sweet limbs hidden in a shroud,
    With spotless lilies on her brow.
        (But tell it not.)

Friend, there are ways of pain and dread
    To veil youth's dawn in sad eclipse ;
She could not see the *poison spread*
    On my pale cheeks and livid lips !
        (But tell it not.)

UNE BONNE FORTUNE.

A MOOD OF MADNESS.

As fretful swords wear out their sheaths by pressure,
   As honey-laden bees grow sick from cloy,
So ardent youth by soft excess of pleasure
   Grows weary of an oft-repeated joy.

'Tis rare to sip the myrrh of love's caresses,
   Godlike to feel a passion in its strength,
But lips that kiss now gold, now raven tresses,
   Must ever yearn for something new at length.

It would be sweet, when slumbers have allayed me,
   To wake from dreams that never knew alarms,
And find, while cold and ghostly thrills invade me,
   Some vague and unknown Presence in my arms.

To feel each rapturous kiss grow strangely colder,
   To breathe the fetor of unearthly breath,
And, with delighted eyes, upon my shoulder
   To see the sweet and lovely face of Death !

December 18, 1876.

1755.

Lisbon, enamored of her beauty, lay
    Girt with a rosary of fragrant flowers ;
    Sun-loved and radiant in a maze of bowers,
She dreamed the idle Summer hours away.

In grateful mood, in shy, coquettish play,
    She called the Spirits and mysterious Powers,
    That guard and beautify her with their dowers,
To come and share her soft, eternal May.

Then the earth trembled, and the flawless sky
    Grew black with ominous shadows of despair,
      While tall towers tottered in a sudden flame !
A fiery hurricane of hell swept by,
    And in an utter darkness everywhere,
      With death and doom, the awful spirits came !

RAVAILLAC SPEAKS.

A MOOD OF MADNESS. 1600.

The world is old and I am young.
　　My tongue
Talks after others who have wrought
　　Their thought
From tissues of fast speeding time,
　　In rhyme
Or prose, and who were great and strong
　　In song.
I come and am unjudged, unknown,
　　Alone ;
Aching my share of hate to earn,
　　And learn
The secrets of mysterious life,
　　Now rife
With wondrous changes of all kind.
　　My mind
Burns to attain some perfect goal,
　　For soul

Have I, and will, with strength and heart.
  The smart
Of life is horrible to bear;
  No prayer
Can ease the torment of its spleen;
  Half lean,
Half fat, my wretched slice I suck.
  Ill luck
Or good I swallow, heedless, rash;
  And dash,
With hopeful feet, unerring, fast,
  Far past
The poisons that the hours instill
  To kill.
I feel the world's tricks and its guiles,
  False smiles;
The worth of woman and of man
  I span.

I do not care if others laugh,
  Or quaff
Rare wines, or if they moan, or weep,
  Or sleep.
I 've seen enough my mind to cloy
  Of joy;

Am sick of friendship, love and lust.
    I thrust
My curses, bitterer than gall,
    On all.
I strive alone for other peace,
    Release
From all the bitterness of life.
    The strife
'Twixt good and evil is unfair,
    And prayer
Is not so soothing as one thinks ;
    The stinks
Of vice fill life, of acrid scent
    And blent
With hellish harmonies that tempt.
    Exempt
No man is, and the soul will sin ;
    Begin,
Eschew wrong first and I 'll adore ;
    Implore
Your gods for proof, should I believe
    And grieve.

I know the value of a tear ;
    Each year

Brings me new proof ; I grow more wise ;
    Mine eyes
See through the darkness and the night.
    More light
Beyond, beyond, by fancy seen,
    Rich sheen
I can descry ; and I am glad,
    Yet sad,
To say that on this gallful earth,
    Where birth
Was given me, I now love to dwell ;
    To tell
That though I can not bend the rod
    Of God,
Or learn the lesson from above
    To love,
That I can curse each living thing,
    And sing
Of hideous days, and horrid nights,
    Their blights,
And all the essences of sin
    Therein ;
Gall mixed with tears, and tears with blood
    And mud ;

And viperous loves as has a fiend,
            For, screened
By callousness, I curse the hour
            And power
That brought me to this hopeless hell
            To dwell.
And yet I have an eager greed,
            A need,
Like famished beasts that growl for food ;
            My mood
Is chronic, and I hope to live
            And give
It rest, ere I shall dwindle by
            And die.

The ages of the world, untold,
            Are old ;
Nations of splendor and of pride
            Have died ;
Cities have filled the world with dread,
            Now dead ;
Great men whom multitudes adored,
            Ignored
By us, have lived in every clime,
            Their time ;

Yet I am jubilant to learn
  My turn
Has come upon this stupid sphere
  To sneer.
My better blood doth quicker flow
  To know
I have not come on earth too late
  To hate ;
And to the waiting worms I 'll bring
  The King !

THE APOSTLE.

A. D. 100.

Barefoot and sore, from Orient lands he came
    Great error-tainted Rome to see and save,
    And urge the incestuous empress and her slave
By God-inspirèd words that burn like flame.

He came their pagan infamy to tame,
    To shield pale martyrs from the beasts that rave
    Upon the Coliseum's sands, and brave
To speak of Christ and tinge their brows with shame.

The monster town that lawless pleasure felt
    Listened and chuckled at his words divine,
      While Cæsar's minions led him thence afar
To vile ignoble slums, where harlots dwelt,
    There to abjure, and left him clogged with wine,
      Shrieking foul oaths in Flora's lupenar !

1877.

MICHAEL DMITRIEVITCH SKOBELEFF.

OBIIT 1882.

The lion is dead, and Prussia now can breathe
  A little span before her doom draws nigh.
  She will not hear thy gallant battle-cry,
Nor will she see thy glittering sword unsheathe.

But thy armed spirit will to the Russ bequeath
  Its pristine valor that can never die,
  While thy brave grenadiers go hurrying by
Their blades in German carrion to seethe.

Dead art thou not, oh, warrior ! For thy name,
  Thy prowess and the memory of thy deeds
    Live indestructible through the Czar's domain ;
And, in some murderous battle's din and flame,
  'Mid sabered Hessians and bewildered steeds,
    Thy turbulent ghost shall find its sphere again !

FAITHFUL.

Supple and cruel as a languid snake
  That awes a linnet with dull eyes of flame,
  Thou lurest me by the magic of thy shame
To throw my life away for thy foul sake !

With lawless vice thy ignoble instincts ache,
  And, Borgia-like, imperious, untame,
  Thy soul, to gain its ignominious aim,
Would fain in blood some chaste existence take.

Pale incest stamps its horror on thy brows,
  Red murder gleams in thy rebellious eyes,
    And throes erotic thy base passions thrill.
No pity an outraged world for thee allows,
  The scaffold claims thy carrion as prize,
    But what is that to me? *I* love thee still !

A MEETING.

"There is no God," I arrogantly cried ;
  "God is a myth, a fable, a disgrace !
Why in His boundless spaces doth He hide?
Where are His might eternal and His pride?
  Where "—*then I suddenly met him, face to face !*

A SULTAN'S WHIMS.

She has perfumed the flow of her hair
With the oil of the attar-gul rare,
  And the flowers that are dear to me ;
She has tinted her lashes with khol,
And she waits for the muezzin to toll,
  For the hour to be near to me.

She has bathed her white body in nard,
And the sleek, yellow hide of a pard
  Warms the delicate feet of her ;
While the lily and rose of her breast
By the glow of the moon are caressed,
  In the beauty complete of her !

All her turban's rich, delicate furls
She has studded with orient pearls,
  Where the gems of her crescent are ;
And has cut with her Alep blade's tip,
To make redder, the red of her lip
  Where my kisses incessant are !

A SULTAN'S WHIMS.

She is clad in a shimmer of sheen,
In a dolman of gold damascene,
  Starred with emeralds numberless.
On a divan of cashmere she lies,
With impatient, black flashings of eyes,
  Of black passion-eyes slumberless.

Both her wee hands, of princess and fay,
Have been tipped to the nail in henneh,
  To delight and charm me with ;
While her slaves, with curved scimitars bare,
Pace, with slow, cat-like tread, here and there,
  As a jest to alarm me with !

From the satin and silk of her kiosk
She dreams out to the moon-glamored bosk,
  As she waits till I come to her ;
While the songs of the bulbul arise,
And the wail of the soft lute replies,
  And the sad guzlas thrum to her.

From her palace, invading the dusk,
Floats a subtle, soft odor of musk,
  And her sighings ascend with it ;

While the murmurs of millions of flowers,
From the mazes of fountains and bowers,
　　Seem in silence to blend with it.

As she waits mid the perfumes that swarm,
The checked passion that darts through her form
　　Burns resistless and comet-like ;
For her love there is no Rhamadán,
And no fasting, no faith, no Korán,
　　No tame passions, Mahomet-like !

＊　　＊　　＊　　＊　　＊

She may wait by the moon, and may dream,
But to-night, to her splendor supreme,
　　My soul dares not be dutiful.
I have given the love that she craves
To Al-Leila, the pearl of her slaves ;
　　To Al-Leila, the beautiful !

LOVE ETERNAL.

(An Impromptu.)

The flowers will still be springing
From earth's green bed,
Dark storms will still be bringing
Their tale of dread,
And birds will still be singing
When we are dead.

New buds will bloom delightful
Upon our head,
New storms, malign and spiteful,
On earth will spread,
And pain will reign still frightful
When God is dead.

But love alone, supernal,
When two souls wed,
Will live in rapture vernal
On passion fed,
Will live in joy eternal
When death is dead!

IN A SEVILLIAN CLOISTER.

In a Sevillian cloister, old and quaint,
  I wandered once, and saw a picture rare :
  A goddess with sublimities of hair,
Holding a rose-leaf to a suppliant saint.

Her dark and perfect locks without restraint
  Fell on an ample bosom, white and fair,
  And, marveling much, I murmured, half in prayer,
" 'T is but a dream an artist loved to paint ;

A vagrant fancy of a fevered mind."
  For none beheld such glorious tresses shine
    On earth or sea, and they will ne'er be seen !
This I believed, until my eyes did find
  The misty marvel of thy hair divine,
    Fit for the brow of some celestial queen.

NAPOLEON II., DUKE OF REICHSTADT.

Dove that found birth within an eagle's nest,
  Bauble of circumstance and shifting fate,
  Thou wast too young to know thy imperial state,
Before thy marvelous father, foe-oppressed,

Fell like a hero ! And thou hadst not guessed,
  In thy sweet, guileless play, that thou wast great,
  And that his name, with its gigantic weight,
Upon thy weakness was ordained to rest.

When thou in after years, with tears and pain,
  The dazzling records of his deeds supreme,
    With all their pomp and splendor, didst peruse,
How must have passed in thy bewildered brain
  -Fantastic visions, fugitive as a dream,
    Of glorious Jénas and dire Waterloos !

1877.

ALSATIA.

The haughty Prussians proudly tread
Upon the mounds that hold my dead ;
They guard me armed with glittering steel,
Unconscious of my mute appeal ;
In serried lines their hosts advance,
But all my love is still with France.

In vain their hordes my valleys fill ;
In vain they gird the Rhine and Ill
With granite forts and bristling guns ;
In vain these vile and hated ones
With neighing steeds upon me prance,
For all my soul is true to France.

I can recall the days when Rome
Sent legions through the Rhenish foam ;
I fell, and was their Cæsar's thrall,
Yea ! with the other lands of Gaul ;
But, oh ! I dreaded not *his* glance,
Because there was no land of France.

I can recall the stubborn fight
Of Ariovistus, king by right,
Who, with his brave, untutored hordes,
Was stricken by the Roman swords.
They left full many a shield and lance
Upon the soil God made for France.

The Alemanni seized me then
With howling hosts of bearded men ;
But Frankish warriors swiftly came
To ravish me with iron and flame.
I heard their grand, defiant chants,
And all my spirit burned for France.

Great Duke Adelrie o'er me reigned,
And by the highest heaven ordained,
His sweet Odilla, without taint,
Became my patroness and saint.
My fields were merry with the dance,
And all my soul went forth to France.

The long years grew ; I lived to share
The mighty empire of Lothaire,
And then for centuries my charms
Were guarded by Teutonic arms.

They toiled upon my soil like ants,
But all my soul was true to France.

Then came a dictate from the throne,
King Louis claimed me as his own.
The hireling troops were stricken down,
Deep in my rebel Rhine to drown ;
Yea, and to-day my spirit pants
With deathless memories of France.

Then plenty and sweet peace were mine.
Ruled by great kings of right divine,
I lived for many bounteous years
Free from oppression and from tears.
I felt no more the German lance,
And all my love went forth to France.

Alas ! there came a day of pain,
When German bandits seized again
My fertile hills, and hold them now,
Staining the beauty of my brow.
In countless legions they advance,
But all my soul is true to France.

The day is near when France will claim
My captive soil with fire and flame.
The foreign jailors that are mine
Will feed the fishes of the Rhine ;
And until God this blessing grants,
My heart and soul are true to France.

TO-DAY, DELICIOUS AGNES, BLONDE AND FAIR

To-day, delicious Agnes, blonde and fair,
  In humble ways I reverently greet
  Thy youth that blossoms in woman's grace complete,
Crowned by the golden glory of thy hair.

In thy deep eyes of blue, intense and rare,
  My sad and musing spirit loves to meet
  A soul whose essence is sublime and sweet,
Soft as the breath of dawn, and pure as prayer.

And when on thee in ravishment I gaze,
  Vague dreams my wandering fancy will surprise ;
    Visions of Phidias and his unfound goal !
And I, too timid e'er to speak or praise,
  Think that I do behold in modern guise
    Some white Greek statue that enshrines a soul.

THE EXECUTIONER'S DREAM.
1793.

Accurse me not, oh, God! and from my forehead
    Avert the world's disdains ;
Thou who dost know how anguishful and horrid
    To me the midnight wanes,
And how in sleep my harrowed soul of pains
    Dreams of red rains !

Each night in the hot terror of my dreaming,
    Swooning with utter dread,
I see the fiends of memory round me teeming,
    Around my guilty bed ;
And trunkless heads e'er flit before me, dead,
    Loathsome and red !

Those hateful heads, the heads that I have sundered,
    Draw near unto me — near
On each dark night, as I have lain and wondered,
    In trembling and in fear.
Some murmur awful secrets in my ear,
    Horrid to hear !

Around me in a buzzing cloud they haunt me,
    Those heads of clotted gore ;
They sing, they weep, they laugh, they sob and taunt me;
    Some shriek, and some implore ;
Oh, God ! They come to curse me more and more
    Than e'er before.

Some kiss me with their clammy lips all gory,
    Some cling to me and bite ;
Oh, severed heads ! is this your martyr-glory,
    To desecrate the night ?
Why in my torture take ye such delight,
    Oh, fiends of fright?

I swoon beneath their putrid, foul caresses ;
    New heads keep swarming still ;
They brush my face with cold and bloody tresses,
    And sometimes whisper shrill,
" Was it my crime if I was forced to kill
    Against my will ? "

I see them in the pale, sad moonlight flitting,
    In dreams of wild despair ;
I feel the icy contact of their spitting
    Upon my brows and hair ;
They never stop nor cease, but through the air
    Float everywhere !

They bite aside the drapery of my curtain,
    With white teeth keen,
And in the ghostly, flickering light, uncertain,
    I see them o'er me lean,
Murmuring constantly, with voice of spleen,
    La Guillotine !

One brings between her teeth her wedding casket,
    With costly gems inlaid ;
Another asks me have I changed my basket,
    And have I oiled the blade ;
Another scoffs and tells me, undismayed,
    I never prayed !

The flesh of every latest victim winces
    Fresh from the reeking knife ;
Soldiers and dukes, ladies and lords, and princes,
    With unearthly strife,
Demand some news of mistress, friend or wife,
    And howl for life.

As day appears my shattered sense grows bolder ;
    I calm my ghostly fears ;
But dream again that, nestled on my shoulder,
    A bleeding head appears ;
Its cold mouth smells of maggots and of biers,
    And at me leers.

I see a head among all others swimming,
        The swan-like neck still wet ;
The eyes with gentle tears are over-brimming ;
        The lips are crimson yet ;
The rare and regal head none can forget,
        Of Antoinette !

It still retains its proud, patrician beauty,
        And soft, silk tresses brown ;
It tells me with a sigh I did my duty,
        And then it looketh down ;
The head still wears a blood-bespattered crown,
        And does not frown.

Unto my lips one head with signs of gladness
        And strangest fervor clings ;
It gazes on my trembling form with sadness ;
        Oh, God ! at times *it sings !*
I note its august brow of sufferings ;
        It is the King's !

Protect me, angels, from the cruel staring
        Of countless angry eyes ;
Protect my soul from their delirious glaring,
        Those seas of eyes that rise ;
Spare me the horror of my victims' cries,
        And of their sighs !

Accuse me not, Oh, God ! and from my forehead
Avert the world's disdains ;
Thou who dost know how anguishful and horrid
To me the midnight wanes,
And how, in sleep, my harrowed soul of pains
Dreams of red rains !

June 1, 1875.

AGOSTINO SUSINI.

OBIIT 1884.

There was a time when, laureled by sweet fame,
  You stood in youth's magnificence and pride,
  Your glorious tones now charmed, now terrified,
And throngs attentive marveled at your name.

Then the sere autumn of existence came,
  The meed of praise no longer could abide,
  And to the world, estranged and cast aside,
Your artist soul no future praise could claim.

But I remember the triumphant past,
  The charm and splendor of your perfect art,
    When on your brow was shrined all manhood's bloom.
And, as the years pass on, I come at last
  To place, while sorrow thrills me to the heart,
    This humble flower of song upon your tomb.

MARIO.

Art reigned incarnate in thy lofty soul,
   Tuning that voice which was Rubini's peer,
   And whose delicious accents, firm and clear,
Could hold each changing passion in control.

But thou wast greatest in some thrilling *rôle*
   That shook the heart or drew the rebel tear ;
   And memories of thee, forever dear,
Will live and linger now from pole to pole.

Death can not ravish thy eternal fame,
   Nor can it snatch the laurel from thy brow ;
    The ermine of thy life is free of stain,
And, for all time, thy ever-glorious name,
   Shrined in the future, as 't is honored now,
    Will pure, supreme and beautiful remain.

December, 1883.

ROSE-WINDOW.

In Blois Cathedral, shunning care's restraint,
   In twilight hours I oft have sighed, alas !
   When gazing on its wondrous colored glass,
Emblazoned with bright forms of god and saint ;

When, pensive, through the lofty aisles I pass,
   I seem to see a subtle life-tint faint
   Steal o'er their cheeks whene'er the solemn plaint
Of claustral voices chants the vesper mass.

And the strange thought will cling unto my mind,
   How the dead artists, who their charm have made,
   Live in those panes before me, side by side ;
Some as pale martyrs, some apostles kind ;
   All in rare, radiant robes of light arrayed,
     Guarding the shrines their art has beautified.

JUDAS THE SECOND.

His Christ came unto him, and from the pain
   And dismal sloughs of misery and care
   Raised him with friendship saintly and most rare,
Saying, "Be thou my friend, my friend remain."

His Christ did more : He let his hand attain
   Honors he dared not humbly beg in prayer ;
   His sinful past in mercy he did spare,
And to uplift him to a throne did deign !

Then, with the liberal laurels on his brows,
   The gift of one immortal, noble heart,
     Who made irradiant his disgraceful lot,
He, traitor to his country and his vows,
   Betrayed that Master with a devil's art ;
     And hell doth know him now as *Bernadotte !*

1880.

FOR THE JURY TO APPRECIATE.

Callous by sorrow, in affliction strong,
  I never whispered unto alien ears
The dreary, tragic story of my wrong,
  But held it sacred through the bitter years.

With calm, angelic patience did I wait,
  Hoping at last to find some lenient soul,
Some clement victim of unkindly fate
  Who with my dire misfortune might condole.

By chance I met one, calling heaven kind,
  And all the pent-up sluices of my gall
Were opened storm-wise to his lordly mind,
  And, like a weeping child, I told him all.

All, all the hideous mystery of my tale ;
  A poem of hellish horror, strange and grand.
Oh, God ! the words that would have made Christ pale
  Were null and lost, *he did not understand !*

With wild eyes watching his unmoving face,
Breathless, no sign of sympathy I found ;
And, maddened by this unforeseen disgrace,
I shot him as I would have shot a hound.

1877.

PAN IS NOT DEAD.

Poets are always writing everywhere,
  In sonnets and in odes, that *Pan is dead !*
The poor old god, whose syrinx charmed the air,
  For them to heaven, or somewhere else, has fled.
Ten thousand times this falsehood they have said,
  And to repeat it daily they contrive ;
In grievous error they have all been led,
  For we all know that Pan is still alive.

They say that flowerful Greece no more is fair,
  In fact, that it is hideous instead ;
That everything is stale, and flat, and bare,
  Because Pan went to the abode of dread.
They weep and rave about his hornèd head,
  His ibex feet and beard, and ever strive
Reports about his funeral to spread,
  But we all know that Pan is still alive.

In vain in morbid stanzas they declare
  How the god lived, before his spirit sped
To high Olympus, place of peace and prayer,

And tell of all the briny tears they shed
When first at school his piteous fate they read ;
  But all in vain fond fancy thus they drive ;
'T is sad upon their hobby's tail to tread,
  But we all know that Pan is still alive.

ENVOI.

Prince, when you read such poet's lines, beware,
  At wonderful conclusions they arrive ;
They may mythology to tatters tear,
  But we all know that Pan is still alive.

IN A BOOK-STORE.

I met her at the Chadwick ball ;
  We danced till it was ended ;
And never did my mind recall
  A creature half so splendid.
Perhaps my love her charm exalts,
  But I can not determine
Whether she looked when in the waltz
  More sweet than in the German.

My soul was filled with such delight,
  With ecstasy so nameless,
That home I rushed and passed the night
  Scribbling at sonnets aimless.
Some were preposterous, some sublime,
  But all were, in their fashion,
Bold challenges to sense and rhyme,
  And Etna-like in passion.

Alas ! I did not send my thought
  And ravings injudicious,

Although the blush they might have brought
  Unto her cheeks delicious.
In fact, the love at my command
  Had not one trait redeeming ;
I never dared to ask her hand,
  And only wooed her dreaming.

Yet chances numberless I had
  Of timidly proposing,
But always something new forbade
  The words my heart disclosing.
I missed occasions at croquet,
  Three at her cousin's party,
And two one night at Ocean Bay
  While we perused "*Astarte.*"

So, after that entrancing ball,
  I felt that luck had perished,
And mournfully I gave up all
  The happy plans I cherished.
Sad, on Broadway next afternoon,
  I strolled in listless manner,
Humming her most detested tune,
  And smoking an Havana.

I thought my wittiest comrade dull,
  My best friend a deceiver ;
I found new beauty in a skull
  And charms in yellow fever.
I loved to muse on lives o'erthrown
  By hatreds energetic,
And with all crimes and horrors known
  My soul grew sympathetic.

Just then she chanced to pass Grace Church,
  Joyous, alert, vivacious,
And never, though I tried to search,
  Saw I a kirk more gracious.
I knew her by her dainty tread,
  Her *chic* among a million,
Her wondrous eyes, her poise of head,
  And her bottine Sevillian.

Then I, of course, forgot my woes,
  For her sweet smile, transcendent,
Melted my *ennui* as the snows
  Melt by the sun resplendent.
She beckoned me and, like a bird,
  Gayly and blithely chattered,

And, though I did not say a word,
  I was immensely flattered.

She dazed me so by joke and jest,
  And by her mellow laughter,
I left my secret unconfessed
  And put it off till after.
But with impatience waited then
  The time to tell her clearly,
That, of all born and unborn men,
  'T was I who loved most dearly.

In the sweet babel of her talk
  My sighs passed by unheeded ;
But, after a delightful walk,
  I found out what she needed.
"Stop in this book-store," she did cry ;
  "It looks like any other ;
I quite forgot, I came to buy
  Some novels for my mother."

We entered, and among the books
  She moved about delighted,
Finding the best in hidden nooks,
  (She *said* she was near-sighted,)

Pausing to read a line or two
  Of Sindbad or Aladdin,
Or something she was told was new
  From Huxley or from Braddon.

Then with her great alluring eyes,
  As blue as heaven in Zante,
In mute and wondering surprise
  She skimmed through Doré's Dante ;
And said, while passing over " Maud,"
  " I 've worshiped this for ages ;
It is *so* sweet." The little fraud
  Was baptized from those pages !

O'er Dobson's " Vignettes " for a while
  She delicately lingered,
And with a fascinated smile
  The " Cloth of Gold " she fingered.
Then Petrarch's volume met her gaze ;
  She added : " I admire it."
Laura, *mon cher*, deserved this praise ;
  I wish *I* could inspire it.

Then, as she read each loving line,
  And seemed quite interested,

From the top shelf a book divine
  I seized, quite unmolested.
It was a volume which I knew
  Before I dared adore her,
And, with the title full in view,
  I laid it down before her.

For half an hour, at any rate,
  She did not see that cover;
And bitterly I then did hate
  The great Italian lover.
But finally she turned to look,
  Her peerless cheeks grew rosy,
And the bright eyes upon the book
  Read, "*I Promessi Sposi*"!

The hint was a sublime success;
  (How could I thus have tarried?)
Those words alone I have to bless,
  For we are safely married.
And now, within my book-case neat,
  Calmly repose together
My dear Manzoni's works complete,
  All bound in Russia leather.

TO AUSTIN DOBSON.

Upon receiving a volume of his poems.

Across the seas a book by friendly care
Comes with its witty *verve* and fancies rare
   To charm me by sweet lines of nameless grace,
   Woven in dainty ways like Mechlin lace,
Perfect as some old Marquis debonair.

They breathe of Versailles and the Parc aux Cerfs,
Of Pompadour, Sabran and La Vallière ;
   I think I see the artist's dreamy face
      Across the seas.
Watteau of rhyme, he ponders in his chair,
Half Alcibiades and half Voltaire,
   Giving shy fantasy a merry chase,
   While smiling in the muse's warm embrace.
To him, kind winds, my admiration bear
      Across the seas.

TAPESTRY.

Sweet days were those, Oh France, when at my will
   Mine eyes could worship in artistic ease
The prodigies of fancy, toil and skill
   Of thy delicious Gobelin tapestries.

And when the sunlight through the gallery streamed
   Upon the fairy texture, all my soul
Fused with the old mythology, and seemed
   A long-lost fragment of the perfect whole.

Pale, languid nymphs, sporting with merry fauns,
   Beckoned me to them with a mystic charm,
And in those amber, rosy, silken dawns
   My spirit dwelt unconscious of alarm.

I gazed upon them tearfully elate,
   Enraptured by the ever-changing sight ;
And in their midst I found myself in state,
   When the Musée had closed one summer night.

All who with cunning hand had been portrayed,
　Famous in fable, history or lore,
· Crowded around me in the solemn shade,
　Alluring dames, intrepid knights of yore.

From every portion of the world of silk
　Descended goddesses and chatelaines ;
Kings on emblazoned palfreys, white as milk ;
　Stalwart crusaders, Jewish slaves in chains.

Looking upon me with large, curious eyes,
　Achilles, with his god-like forehead bare,
Whispered in Greek, with accents of surprise,
　Some eager words to blonde La Vallière.

Bluff Charles Martel, with battle-axe and shield,
　Pointed me out to Harry of Navarre ;
And, led by Cupids from some blooming field,
　Cleopatra's glance fell on me like a star !

The august Louis, fourteenth of the name,
　Powdered and wigged, deigned for a time to scan
My modern face, that burned with conscious shame,
　And gave opinions to inebriate Pan.

Borgia and Phryne, both on pleasure bent,
 Laughed at my novel raiment for awhile ;
And behind Pharaoh's diamond-studded pschent
 I saw Du Barry's pink, bewitching smile.

Saladin, arm and arm with Luther, came,
 One with his scimitar, one with his book ;
And on my palpitating, ravished frame
 The fair Madonnas cast a pitying look.

Before my eyes Prometheus, unbound,
 Kissed the gemmed hand of Marie Antoinette,
While the grim vulture, harmless on the ground,
 Flapped its great wings and timed their minuet.

Ninon de l' Enclos courted Cæsar's youth ;
 Hector to Pompadour wild wars rehearsed,
And in surprise I heard the Biblic Ruth
 Merrily chat with Huss and Charles the First.

Snake-haired Medusa smiled on Huguenots ;
 Agnes Sorel praised Bayard's mighty strength ;
Nero escorted Mary Queen of Scots ;
 Moses propounded creeds with Leo Tenth !

All passed in flesh and blood before my sight,
One miracle of beauty most supreme ;
Oh, cruel sun ! how I despised thy light,
That proved to me that all was but a dream !

1881.

BAUDELAIRE.

Âme puissante en deuil ! tes haines frémissantes
  Ont peuplé ton esprit de sujets monstrueux ;
Les cauchemars affreux de tes nuits effrayantes
  Viennent baver leur sang d' un noir enfer hideux.

L' Ennui ronge ton coeur, et les voix éclatantes
  Des archanges divins, aux doux yeux radieux,
Ne sauraient t' éloigner de tes noires amantes,
  La Mort ! et le Dégout ! poëte merveilleux !

Ta Muse, au front rêveur, qui rugit et qui brâme,
  Répond en ricanant à ce monde irrité,
Que le " Laid c' est le Beau," que le Laid est une âme,
  Et ta rime de feu, pleine d' autorité,
Sait montrer à nos yeux aveugles et rebelles
Que la fange contient choses chastes et belles.

1875.

FOUR SONNETS.

I.—ADELINA PATTI.

La noche, cuando oi tu voz divina,
 El limpio canto y el immortal accento,
 He comprendido el bello firmamento
O casta *Amina*, o graciosa *Adina*.

No tiene angel la voz mas cristalina,
 No tiene pecho human mas sentimiento :
 Dulce con fuerza como el puro viento,
Que llora, piensa, que tambien fulmina.

Cierto, su noble son es un diamante
 Que yo tremblando con placer adoro,
Supremo, grande, claro, triunfante !
 Y, quebrantado y hechizado imploro
A Dios, en su gloria centellante
 Llamarte reina del celeste coro.

II.—FAURE.

J'admire la beauté de ton talent splendide,
 Tu sais comprendre enfin les mystères du cœur,

Sans défaillance aucune et pour ton art avide,
 Tu braves le dédain des ignorantes, sans peur.

L'amour sacré du *vrai* t'inspire et puis te guide,
 De l'inconnu tu sais découvrir la valeur ;
Car c'est toi *nelusko*, c'est toi *Juan* perfide,
 C'est toi le fier *Pietro*, c'est toi *Hamlet* rêveur !

Mais quand je vois ton nom, de douloureux regrets
 M'accablent, car je pense aux jours qui sont passés,
 Les jours ensoleillés de ta jeunesse heureuse,
Le temps si glorieux de tes plus beaux efforts,
 Car le divin Mozart et le grand Gluck sont morts
 Sans avoir entendu ta voix mélodieuse !

III.—SANTLEY.

The northern blood that courses through thy frame
 Is warm and passionate with a southern fire,
 And ever prompt to strengthen and inspire
The nobler efforts which thy soul could claim.

We feel its subtle presence, and admire
 Thy march triumphant from an artist's aim
 Up to the distant, dizzy heights of Fame,
Thy goal, thy ultimatum, thy desire !

Yea, and thou hast not swerved, thou hast not turned ;
Straight to the end over the cheerless ground
Thou hast made progress worthy of thy dream,
And now, when stragglers on Art's path are spurned,
Thou standest resolute with thy laurels crowned,
And, of thy future, arbiter supreme !

IV.—MARIO.

Artista degno d'ogni gloria e onore,
Tu sei il Dio del sublime canto
Havvi nella tua voce il riso e il pianto
L'idillio ameno e i gridi di furore.

Il sentimento nato nel tuo cuore
E inver delizioso, quasi santo,
E noi t'amiamo d'un ardor cotanto
Che mettiamo in oblio ogni dolore.

Edgardo, Fausto, Lionel, Elvino,
Sono i giojelli della tua corona
L'emulo sei di Duprez, di Rubini
E anzi o favorito del destino,
Nella tua voce vive, grida e suona
L'anima colossale del Salvini.

CHINOISERIE.

A la Princesse Tung-Chwâ-Hlin.

Je voudrais être ton miroir,
    Et le soir,
Refléter tes yeux, noirs et doux,
   Quand tu te mires, ma charmante
    Indolente,
  Sur ton lit de bambous.

Ah ! je voudrais être le vent
    Languissant,
  Faisant frémir ton éventail ;
  Ou bien la coupe d'or qui baise,
    À son aise,
   Tes lèvres de corail,

Ah ! que ne suis-je Mandarin,
    Fort, hautain,
A trois dragons d'or singuliers ;
Pour oser te surprendre en traitre
    Puis en maître,
  Baiser tes petits pieds.

Que ne suis-je l'esclave noir,
    Qui le soir
Vient parfumer tes bleus cheveux ;
Ou bien le suave k'hol qu'il passe,
    Avec grâce,
  Sous tes yeux langoureux !

Que ne suis-je le colibri
    Êbloui,
Qui te réveille le matin,
Baisant d'amour, quand il se penche
    Ta main blanche
  Comme le Kaolin !

Ou bien encor, le brodequin,
    Si mutin,
Qui chausse ton blanc pied d'enfant,
Ou le pur attár-gul qui tombe,
    Ma colombe,
  Sur ton corps ravissant !

Dans les beaux jardins de Pékin,
    Et Nankin,
En babillant avec les fleurs,

Je fais pour te plaire des odes
Aux Pagodes,
Et je cache mes pleurs.

J'écoute quand dans ton palais
D'or et jais,
Tu prends ta Yue-Kin le matin,
Et ta voix d'oiseau qui m'enchante,
Et qui chante,
Notre Buddhâ divin.

Rose de Chine, Fleur de Thé,
Je serai
À toi fidèle pour toujours.
Mon âme fuit parmi les ombres
Des bois sombres
Pour chérir ses amours.

Je t'aime et je te suis, hélas,
Pas à pas,
Mais ton coeur ne sait qu'oublier,
A ! si je meurs, quand la nuit tombe,
Sur ma tombe,
Viens un instant pleurer.

LES MOUSQUETAIRES.

Le premier à l'assaut, vrai Bayard du carnage !
  Au sourire rêveur, à l'éloquente voix,
Pourfendant les Anglais, ferraillant avec rage,
  Type des anciens preux, noble *Athos*, je te vois.

Salut, beau *d'Artagnan*, superbe de vaillance,
  Armé de pied en cap sur ta maigre jument,
L'oeil vif et le front haut, cherchant insolence
  Criant, " Mordious, Messieurs, mettez flamberge au vent"!

Et toi, naïf *Porthos*, aux combats téméraire,
  Au doux coeur chaleureux, à l'invincible main,
Je t'entends grommeler de ta voix de tonnerre,
  Ah ! ça maître hotelier ! qu'on m'apporte du vin !

Salut bel *Aramis*, adoré des marquises,
  Qui fait si bien la cour et le sonnet galant,
Quel chic dans tes duels, quelles façons exquises,
  Mousquetaire coquet, gentil abbé fringant.

1876.

LA BLASÉE.

Dans son boudoir Watteau, l'indolente Marquise,
  Agace de son pied mutin, blanc et mignon,
  Le museau moite et noir de son petit bichon,
Tout en baillant un peu d'une façon exquise.

Pour fuir le *spleen* naissant, Madame alors devise,
  " Si je lisais Balzac ? . . *bah !* ça m'énerve . . . non . . .
  Pour charmer mes ennuis Gautier n'a plus le don,
Mais que faire mon Dieu ? pauvre femme incomprise !

Gounod est insipide, et j'éxècre Verdi,
Encore un peu, ma foi, j'aimerais mon mari,
  S'il venait consoler sa blonde délaissée ;
  C'est drôle tout de même être ainsi désœuvrée.
Vraiment je n'y comprends rien, *rien* absolument,
Et pourtant j'ai changé ce mois deux fois d'amant !

1887.

LE MARQUIS DE SADE.

Sublime libertin ! qu'on nomme à tort immonde,
   J 'admire tes hauts faits ; esclave du désir,
   Tu ravageais Paris pour pouvoir assouvir
Tes fières passions, ta verve furibonde.

Pour toi, tout était bon, Marguerite ou Joconde,
   Tes sens voluptueux ne savaient point dormir ;
   Et, pour un amour vil, un bizarre soupir,
Ton cœur aurait voulu bouleverser un monde !

La douce vierge brune, ou la blonde marquise,
   Les catins du trottoir, et les dames d'atours,
Ont reçu tes baisers, Roi de la paillardise !
Frère en péché, merci, de ton secret infâme,
   Jes sais enfin créer ces sublimes amours,
Qui font vibrer ma chair et rayonner mon âme !

PAUL HAMILTON HAYNE.

Je suis émerveillé, ta splendide carrière,
　O poëte rêveur, apôtre de la foi !
　L'Art pur et la Beauté font ta divine loi ;
Au doute tentateur tu sais crier " arrière"!

Comme le grand Hugo, dans ta force plénière,
　Bien loin du monde aimé qui t'acclamerait roi,
　Tu cherches l'Idéal, en exil comme toi,
Et rien n'a pu flétrir ton âme chaste et fière.

Triste mais courageux, sans peur, sans défaillance,
　Tu caches à nos yeux les fièvres de tes nuits ;
Quand ton cœur dit *Néant*, ta voix dit *Espérance.*
　Hélas, ami, je sens tes immenses ennuis ;
Tu chantes noblement, penché sur un abîme,
Et j'aime et je comprends ton dévoûment sublime !

6 Novembre, 1878.

PIZZICATO.

Pinçant du doigt la mandoline,
   Je veux chanter jusqu' à demain,
   Car j'aperçois ta blanche main,
Soulevant la rouge courtine.

Si j'ai froid, mon âme est en feu,
   Et que m'importe la nuit sombre ?
   Je vois briller à travers l'ombre
Comme une étoile ton œil bleu.

Tu te penches tremblant encore . . . . .
   Ta duègne doit être endormie,
   Allons ! du courage, ma mie,
Laisse tomber l'échelle d'or !

O ! brune fleur de Barcelone,
   Pourquoi me fais-tu tant languir ?
   Je veux baiser, ou bien mourir,
Tes roses lèvres de Madone !

TO H. W. LONGFELLOW.

Sonetto composto pel nobile Signor Enrico W. Longfellow, dopo aver letto il suo Capo lavoro " Il Ponte Vecchio di Firenze."

SONETTO.

Scritto hai di luoghi al cor Toscano santi,
    Dell' Arno e di Santa Maria Del Fiore,
D'Amalfi tutta rose ed amaranti,
    Di Roma augusta in tutto il suo splendore !

Rifulge Italia d'immortali incanti,
    Nei versi che t'inspira ardente il core ;
E le sue glorie, i pregi, i prieghi, i pianti,
    Trovano un éco in te sempre d' amore !

E della bella Italia tu sei degno,
    Che a te lasció Petrarca l'armonioso
    Plettro d'amor ; Boccaccio il suo sorriso ;
Ma di Danto il sublime e forte ingegno,
    Rese il tuo spirto grande e vigoroso,
    Nè mai il tuo nome fia dal suo diviso !

GAETANO DONIZETTI.

Degno sei tu d 'Italia, o genio santo.
    Fulge il tuo nome in immortal splendore,
    Ed i sospir del tuo celeste cuore
Ai nostri spirti daran sempre incanto.

L' accento tuo, o sia di riso o pianto,
    Sarà pel suol natiò eterno onore,
    Poichè, per te la Musa con amore
Vestissi tutta d 'un novello ammanto.

Gl' inspirati concenti di *Lucia*,
    Prova de genio e di preclara mente,
Riviveranno in rimembranza pia
    Di te chi festi elettrizzar la gente !
        Saranno un letto di olezzanti fiori,
        Perpetueranno insiem gloria ed onori !

À T. B. ALDRICH.

Grand poëte amoureux de la beauté puissante,
  Votre âme peut créer un fier accent vainqueur,
Pour chanter dignement d'une voix enivrante
  Les fortes passions, la grâce et la douceur.

Partout dans vos beaux vers la muse nous enchante,
  Et, captivés, émus, par leur pure splendeur,
Nous savons y trouver, ô surprise charmante,
  L'exquise originalité de votre cœur !

Poëte, pour ces dons vous êtes adoré,
Et toujours, quand je lis, ébloui, pénétré,
Un de vos chants ailés et doux comme un mystère,
  J'entends du haut du ciel un murmure, et je vois
  Gautier, tout souriant, qui de sa noble voix
Vous dit, "Béni sois-tu, mon bien-aimé, mon frère !"

19 Mars, 1881.

"LA DUBARRY."

A Rose of Song, Plucked from the Guillotine and the Pillory of History.

Quand dans Paris ton charme étrange,
Fille adorable, fut connu,
Comme étant ton droit et ton dû,
La ville te baptisa "l' Ange."
De tes amants tu faisais fi,
O, gracieuse Dubarry !

Quand à la cour étincelante
De Louis, le Roi Bien Aimé,
Reine de grâce et de beauté,
Tu vins, belle enfant rayonnante,
Son coeur royal fut ébloui,
O, sémillante Dubarry !

Quand dans son palais, entourée,
Écoutant les propos galants,
Les madrigaux des courtisans,
Qui t' appelaient Madone ou fée,
Ta lèvre a gentiment souri,
Délicieuse Dubarry.

Quand dans ta chambre tapissée,
Bijou de Boucher et Watteau,
Tu grignotais un gros gâteau,
Mignonne gourmande adulée,
Le Roi te trouvait belle ainsi,
Rieuse et folle Dubarry.

Et quand de tes atours parée,
Tu pris ton verre aux soupers fins,
Il aimait de ses blanches mains
Caresser ta gorge adorée,
Le vin le rendait étourdi,
Tu rougissais, o Dubarry !

Pourquoi part-il de son vieux Louvre ?
Où court-il par ce vilain temps ?
Ah, bon ! j'oublie, — tu l'attends,
Il parle bas : — la porte s'ouvre.
Ne crains rien, je suis endormi ;
Discret surtout, ma Dubarry.

Quel charmant règne de folies,
De mouches, sonnets et bichons,
D'amour, de guerre et de chansons,

De langoureuses insomnies :
Ton bon Louis était ravi,
N'est-ce-pas, belle Dubarry !

Hélas, ici tout n'est pas fête,
Les temps sont changés : — il le faut,
On outragea ta blonde tête,
Joyau de roi, sur l'échafaud !
D'angoisse atroce elle a frémi,
Pauvre, innocente Dubarry !

SONNET.

Tu rirais gentiment, coquette jouvencelle,
  Si je te murmurais doucement et tout bas,
Que mon coeur t' appartient, que je te trouve belle,
  Et qu 'un baiser mignon vaudrait un noir trépas.

Ah, oui, tu sourirais, et la brune étincelle
  Jaillirait de tes yeux, si je faisais un pas,
Pourquoi me permets-tu d 'espérer, ma cruelle,
  Quand je t'adore tant, si tu ne m 'aimes pas ?

Ton coeur est donc fermé à triple cadenas ?
  Mais, est-ce bien un coeur ? Non, une citadelle,
Qu' il faut prendre d 'assaut à grand renfort de bras.
  J' en ferai le doux siège, alert, armé, fidèle,
Pour conquérir ton coeur, mais si je tombe, hélas,
  Daigneras-tu panser ma blessure mortelle ?

ENVY.

The imperious sun, grown sullen by great hate,
  Holds in its mighty heart of light and fire
  A wild and uncontrollable desire,
That night can soothe not, nor can time abate.

Dead æons numberless have seen it wait,
  Haughtily patient in its awful ire,
  Hopeless, alas! yet striving to aspire
To goals impossible, as deaf as Fate.

Had it the power to merit one sweet boon,
  Gladly it would forever in gloom eclipse
    The glorious Heaven of light that in it glows,
For it is fain to silver, as did the moon,
  Juliet's delicious and ecstatic lips,
    When resting flower-wise upon Romeo's.

1877.

ORIGINALITY.

Once, as I pondered o'er strange books and sought
  From secrets of the past some knowledge new,
  Within my laboring mind there sudden grew
The perfect germ of a stupendous thought !

No bizarre brain as yet had ever wrought
  This odd, weird wonder into shape, and few
  Could from the store of fancy bring to view
A whim to equal this, to me untaught !

I hailed its brilliant advent with delight.
  But, as I dreamed, I heard a sad voice say :
    " *I, who am living in a spirit home,*
With the *same thought* that pleasures thee to-night
  Charmed grim Tiberius on a festal day,
    And made tumultuous laughter roar through Rome !"

INCONSISTENCY.

Once in the chancel of a church austere,
　　Upon the illumined altar-steps I prayed,
　　While near me knelt, in somber garb arrayed,
Hosts of repenting sinners thrilled with fear.

Without, the tempest swept by, swift and drear,
　　When suddenly a fiery and livid blade
　　Of lightning struck the shining spire, and laid
Its Gothic beauty shattered far and near!

And then the germs of doubt dawned in my soul,
　　Why, if God lived within this house to know
　　　　That suppliants bowed and dared to Him aspire,
Did He, with wrath and wondrous uncontrol,
　　Strike it to dust with His infuriate blow,
　　　　And mar its majesty with avenging fire?

THE MASTERS.

I.—A CIRCUS MASTER SPEAKS TO THE CLOWN.

Come, rouse yourself, ridiculous old clown,
Try to be funny, try to please the town.
    One hundred seats are sold!
    And, tho' you're poor and old,
You're paid enough to cartwheel and to jest,
Come! show your jolly tricks, and be possessed
    Like devils with mad laughter!
    What are you crying after?
Your child is dead? Bah! Jump right in the ring.
A whining clown forsooth's a silly thing.
    Turn twenty hand-springs right away,
    Or else, by God! I'll stop your pay.
Dance all your pain and carrion to the grave,
For all I care—but make the people rave.
    Click! Clack! (*Snaps his whip.*)

II.—GOD SPEAKS TO THE EARTH.

Awake, and be submissive to my powers,
Cover thyself again with ferns and flowers.

How dost thou dare to dream
Infecund, where, supreme,
I bid thee roll incessantly and work?
Can fancies mutinous in thy nothing lurk?
Produce, and bow before me,
Create, bring forth, adore me.
Slavishly give to men both balm and bane.
Let naught forgotten be of woe and pain,
Else I will visit thee with fire,
My malediction and my ire.
Revolve, vile earth, and, silent as the grave,
Obey me, for thou art my thing, my slave!
Click! Clack!

IT WERE TOO TAME.

A MOOD OF MADNESS.

It were too tame my hated foe to kill !
   I fain would drug him in such subtle ways,
   That sullen Death my handiwork would praise,
   That friends who guarded him thro' hopeless days
Should never know that he was living still.

The livid, flawless pallor of his face
   Would leave no sign of potent poison sipped,
   When in his bands and flowing shroud equipped,
   He should be laid in the ancestral crypt,
The last vile scion of a lawless race.

And I would be there in the close, cold gloom,
   When all had gone, and, with dilated eyes
   Leering in rapture at my cherished prize,
   Would calmly wait to hear his hellish cries
For mercy when he wakened in the tomb.

What grander vengeance could my injury claim
   Than there to hear his agonizing groan,
   The frantic effort in the dark alone,
   The supplicating pleas, the maddening moan,
And thro' the coffin crack to shriek my name?

Ah! then to say, "I pity thy sad lot,"
   And of sweet pardon eloquently speak.
   Oh, somber joy, delicious and unique,
   While his low, airless sighs grew faint and weak,
To draw *one* nail, give hope — *but open not!*

July, 1877.

DELUDED.

I pity all whose superstitions need
   Perpetual prayer vague terrors to allay ;
   Poor trembling bigots who, till they turn gray,
Place fervent trust in some unworthy creed.

Dreading a phantom hell, they meekly plead,
   The crafty priest religiously obey,
   And think by genuflections night and day,
That God will for their frailties intercede !

Fools ! when the world is but an atom rolled
   Amid the starry vastness of dim space,
     This vain and miserable human chaff,
With confidence derisive to behold,
   Dreams that to Heaven ascend its cries for grace,
     And can not hear God's cold, contemptuous laugh.

POSTHUMOUS SELF-RESTRAINT.

Were I to lie below some marble tomb,
　In cold decay, forgotten of mankind
In the foul quiet and eternal gloom,
　Such utter peace my weary bones would find,

That, should a gentle spirit to me come,
　Seeing me there, cadaverous and stark,
And tell me in my startled torpor, numb
　With awful whispers in the awful dark,

That it had loved me and possessed the power,
　God-given and rare, to animate my clay,
That if I chose, I could in one brief hour
　Find sweetest life again and go my way,

I, in my coffin's darkness and disgrace,
　Sure of its power the promise to fulfill,
Would closer wrap the shrould around my face,
　And with contempt unspeakable lie still.

1878.

SATISFACTION,

Men, tranced by beauty, pause and gaze upon
  The azure-starred sublimity of night,
  Or watch with moods of wondering delight
The shifting clouds that veil a dying sun.

They think of all the good the Lord hath done
  In the stern calm of His eternal might,
  And hardened sinners marvel at the sight
Of luminous spheres that move since time begun.

Ravished and mute, with eager eyes, they stand,
  Feeling new awe within their spirit blend,
    And of unending praise their lips are loud,
While, far above them, infinite and grand,
  God hears this homage to the throne ascend,
    And of his work is insolently proud.

ANANKÉ.

A tree is blooming in some distant grove,
  A mammoth oak whose branches pierce the sky,
Peopled with birds, where agile squirrels rove,
  Where owlets hoot and where the eagles die.

A maid is seated in a dreary room,
  Her drearier thoughts are far, ah ! far away,
While, with a heart immersed in utter gloom,
  She wears a cerement till the close of day.

Fair flowers are sleeping in the frozen ground,
  Until spring beckons them with signs unseen
To aid the glory of new nature crowned,
  And, starlike, light the meadows' dewy green.

A block of marble in a quarry lies,
  Inert, unfeeling in its silent sleep,
While o'er it, roaring thro' the somber skies,
  The wintry winds their doleful vigils keep.

From that same tree my coffin will be wrought,
  Kind hands will place those flowers upon my head,
The maiden's work will be the shroud I sought,
  The marble block will hold me with the dead.

1889.

HENRI DE LA ROCHEJAQUELEIN.

At the Battle of Chemillé, April 11th, 1793.

I.

Soldiers ! Though yonder fiery flood should swallow me,
I, true, will fight for France,
And when you see me for her sake advance,
Follow me !

II.

Soldiers ! With joy yon deadly squares can thrill me,
I scorn their sabered might,
And should I turn or waver in the fight,
Kill me !

III.

And should a bullet with their corpses range me,
And leave me gashed or dead,
Soldiers, by God's omnipotence o 'erhead,
Avenge me !

March, 1889.

MOON SPLEEN.

Doomed by a cruel god to pine alone,
  Chaste and serene, in continents of space,
  I weary of gazing on the Earth's dull face,
Whose secrets since creation I have known.

I can recall the blond glow I have thrown
  Where Babylon reared its grandeur and its grace,
  And over pillared Karnac I can trace
Dead rays that linger on immortal stone.

But, ah ! the glories of Neronian Rome
  And templed Greece are sweet no more to me !
  I tire of lending light to mart and dome,
And loath the palpitant splendors of the sea ;
  While desolate, in my star-encompassed home,
  I roam forever in my white *ennui*.

THE TOWER OF BABEL SPEAKS.

In ways unknown to mortals, I regret
    The memory of that grand and haughty hour,
    When the symmetric insolence of my tower
Awed the pale heaven that braves my anger yet.

No stone of mine now crumbling can forget
    My palm-clad pomp in those sweet days of power,
    When my colossal summit made stars cower
And shrink before my awful silhouette.

Oh! despicable, puny hordes of men!
    When I held sky and space within my reach,
      What souls had ye thus to be overcome?
Why did your coward hands desert me, when
    Jehovah, in his wrath, had blent all speech?
      Could ye not work, oh, fools! though ye were dumb?

1878.

IS LIFE WORTH LIVING?

If we could rub Aladdin's lamp each day,
   And at our palm attentive genii find
   To grant our every whim and wish resigned ;
Yea ! could we lure the golden goose to lay

A precious egg that we might keep alway ;
   And had we wishing-mantles round us twined,
   Or Fortunatus's rare wallet lined,
And youth's elixir to avert decay,—

Then life, perchance, might sweet and pleasant be.
   Who knows ?   Such magic might delight us much,
      Yet we, perhaps, might yearn for something more.
We would find qualms and deem ourselves unfree,
   Find life obnoxious to the light and touch,
      And dream and doubt, dejected as before !

WINDS.

The Night has girdled on her garb of glooms,
  The bleak north wind shrieks shrill along the air,
While startled clouds are tossed afar like plumes,
  And stricken forests shiver in despair.

Out on the heaving ocean, vast and dark,
  The mad storm drives, with swift, succeeding shocks
And angry hiss, a frail and mastless bark
  To utter doom upon the expectant rocks.

*   *   *   *   *

Heavy with spice, and languorous with calm,
  The soft south wind, fresh from gold tropic seas,
Caresses with delicious wafts of balm
  The summer splendor of the Antilles.

It seeks amid the emerald of its bowers
  The hammock where a Creole, pale and fair,
Lies like a flower among the other flowers,
  And plays with the soft splendors of her hair.

COMEDY.

Oh, bitter life !   Unsufferable task,
　When some poor mime to earn his daily bread
Must play the clown, or don the Thespian mask,
　And hide with *rouge* the tears he may have shed.

Some see their rival with a loved one strain
　Exulting eyes to watch their suffering,
And, while swift jealousy fires every vein,
　Repeat an odious rôle, or laugh and sing.

The favorite actor, by the mass loved best,
　Makes his *entrée* while thronged admirers cheer ;
Alas ! they see not Death in every jest,
　His low, consumptive cough they can not hear.

The girl whose grace and art cause such delight,
　Praised for her charming ways and dainty tread,
Smiles sweetly still, but know you how, last night,
　With tearful eyes she mourned her mother, dead ?

No, no ! The very man you have preferred,
   Whose tragic power among the best is styled,
May think as *Hamlet, Lear,* or *Richard Third,*
   Of dismal garrets and his starving child.

Yet proud, fault-finding critics of the play,
   Carelessly judging without heart or right,
With flippant mien and drawling voice may say,
   "*How badly So-and-So performed to-night.*"

RESURRECTION.

A placid lake dreamed the dull days away
  In Scotland's leafy heart, the wild deer's home,
  Yet never knew the ecstasy of foam,
The curl of waves, or the grim tempest's sway.

But storms encompassed it one fatal day,
  The snaky lightnings o'er its bank did roam,
  And to its sheltering snow-girt cedars clomb,
Stirring the blue depths in wild disarray.

Like that calm lake, my heart serenely dreamed,
  Unconscious of alarm, until you came,
    Leading Love with you, vigorous and free ;
Then the strong lights of passion grandly gleamed,
  My heart arose, new-born, in fear and flame,
    Made by new love one vast and troubled sea !

BIZARRERIE.

Il y a des héros en mal comme en bien.—LaRochefoucauld.

How dull historic page would be
　　If every race were ruled with justice ;
If men in every clime, born free,
Could live in peace, content to see
　　The eventless reign of an Augustus !

How sad, if mild apostles swayed
　　With lenient laws a mighty nation !
If glorious War no longer preyed,
If noble conquests were not made,
　　If hearts possessed no emulation.

How flat the universe would seem
　　Without debauch, and crime, and famine !
Slaughter made grand with glaives that gleam,
Pestilence, outrage, sin supreme,
　　And eager prayers to God and Mammon !

Had the broad world seen such dead time,
　　Had nations died with no offender,

Would we have had grim Dante's rhyme,
Titian unique, Shakespeare sublime,
   And Art in all its vivid splendor ?

No ! The millennium given to man,
   Though sought and begged for through the ages,
From Patagon to Astrakan,
Would please but for a fleeting span,
   And would not crush his Gothic rages !

And all who lived in indolence,
   Bereft of tyrant, god and hero,
Would in their tame magnificence
Rebel, and with desires intense
   Long for a Cæsar or a Nero !

DOST THOU RECALL, MY SWEET ANNETTE?

Dost thou recall, my sweet Annette,
  How hand and hand we went together,
In fragrant fields by soft dews wet,
  And how we kissed below the heather?

Dost thou recall those nights in June,
  That only poets' minds can treasure,
When love's sweet path with flowers was strewn,
  When Hope and Joy were born of Pleasure?

Oh ! such a past can not be mute,
  Such bliss can not be crushed in sorrow,
Although thou art a prostitute,
  And I am to be hanged to-morrow.

THE ELEPHANT.

He strides, majestic, through his vast domain ;
  All India's jungles unto him belong.
  To battle with the pards God made him strong,
And he of his sharp, glittering tusks is vain.

There, sheltered from the sun-fire and the rain,
  Unconscious of the javelin or the thong,
  He thunders forth his wild and wooing song,
When monstrous loves have thrilled his flesh again.

But when I see him, with all courage fled,
  Chained as a captive on an alien ground,
    Far from the torrid pleasaunce of his home,
I think of those great days, forever dead,
  When Hannibal led his ancestry renowned
    To crush the Imperial phalanxes of Rome !

THE OAK.

When in the stately groves, where thou dost bloom,
  I roam and gaze upon thee from below,
  I glory in the grandeur thou dost show,
And even my thoughts thy majesty assume.

The storms of ages and the tempests' gloom
    Have striven in vain to lay thy glory low,
    While starred, serene and wreathed in mistletoe,
Thou giv'st to myriad birds a home or tomb;

And as I mark thy brown and rugged trunk,
    That Gallic lances proudly could defy,
      I dream of those dead days in leafy June,
When, with white trailing robes and visage shrunk,
    The trucculent Druids grimly passed thee by
      With bleeding victims haloed by the moon!

A WOMAN'S WHIM.

Utterly weary of these modern creeds,
  That hail the pain and passion of a cross,
  My doubting soul, that finds in them but dross,
A far more grand and glorious worship needs.

This sempiternal God, that pants and bleeds
  To save mankind, can locks all gory toss,
  Thorn-crowned, superb, but I feel not His loss ;
Such useless martyrdom to my sense ne 'er pleads.

Mahomet's cult, like Manitou's, is tame ;
  Brahma and Buddhâ teach no lofty things ;
    I see a God that can their powers eclipse,
And long in some wild chaos of sacred flame
    To seek sweet shelter under Satan's wings,
      And kiss all hell upon his perfect lips !

TO HENRY W. LONGFELLOW.

After Reading His Italian Sonnet to the Old Bridge at Florence.

Thou sing'st of lands dear to the Tuscan heart ;
  Of peerless Arno glittering in dull gold ;
  Of rosy Amalfi, where thy feet have strolled ;
Of Rome's great gloom or of the Pisan mart ;

In thy rare poesy, as perfect as thine art,
  Italy revels in a flawless mold,
  And all her prayers and sufferings manifold
Form of thy theme the supreme nobler part.

For Petrarch's spirit from the dimly grand
  Vague lapse of centuries has thy fancy moved,
    And languid suns Venetian o 'er thee steal.
Italia's glory smiles at thy command,
  While through thy song, which Dante would have loved,
    I hear Boccaccio's silvery laughter peal.

IMPROMPTU BOUT RIME.

The warm sun slants upon a myrtled plain ;
  Brown linnets watch the blue Ilissus flow ;
  Benignant gods their choicest gifts bestow ;
Calm and serene the shifting twilights wane.

The woods are still that heard war's pomp and pain ;
  The silent beaches hide no ships of woe ;
  And Thracian javelins no longer glow
Across the flowery hills like steely rain.

Dead and unvestaled is the temple's fire,
  Flown are the valiant hosts of nobler kind,
    And flown the dream of beauty and of peace ;
No hope, nor hope of hope, no new desire,
  Naught but the drowsy murmur of the wind,
    Through voiceless glens, *and yet this once was Greece.*

1881.

WOMEN.

Were I a woman, I would not pray to be
  The great Semiramis or Joan of Arc,
  The fair Sorel, a Catherine grim and dark,
Or Cleopatra, supple as the sea.

Nor would it in sweet manner pleasure me
  To be fond Juliet listening to the lark,
  Nor yet a Staël, with genius for a mark,
Nay, nor pale Marie Stuart, queen and free.

Had I of such rare transformation choice,
  I would be Messalina, warm and lewd,
    Or amorous Sappho, with wild whims impure.
Yea ! and my lawless spirit would rejoice
  To live in white Dubarry's bosom nude,
    Or on the glittering breast of Pompadour !

A WAY TO KILL.

For lying lips that lent me hope, I wasted
  Years in unmanly dalliance at your feet,
And by false promises of joys untasted,
  I found the infamous abasement sweet.

You spurned my love !   Well, conscious of my blunder,
  I go without reproach, without a sigh,
To seek in Orient lands grim battle's thunder,
  Forget, and in some revel of steel to die.

Courting the hissing bace, the brutal saber,
  My soul to all the glory of war will yield,
And the calm night upon the bloody labor
  Will fall and find one lifeless on the field.

Beneath the warm and eastern sky, star-spangled,
  Half-hidden in the long and gory grass,
Over my livid corpse, all crushed and mangled,
  Great hosts of maddened cavalry will pass !

The iron hoofs will stamp out every feature,
  All, all the luckless face that charmed you not,
Until none recognize a human creature
  In that foul, shapeless mass of blood and rot.

Blessed be the sun upon my carrion falling!
  Blessed be the wind that lulls it! For my soul,
That hovers near it in the gloom appalling,
  Will find at last its vengeance and its goal.

Oh, enviable Death! Supreme perdition!
  God speed the gaunt flies which, with virus sleek,
Born from the hell of my decomposition,
  Will cross far seas to bite your rosy cheek!

July 8, 1877.

BLUE.

Upon the ocean's vivid blue
  A scorching sun hurls down, intense,
One torrid, incandescent hue
  Of anger and malevolence.

Blue is the hot and sultry air,
  Blue are the depths of drowsy waves,
A mad, blind blue falls everywhere,
  And one poor mortal raves

Upon a cracking raft alone,
  With throbbing throat and palsied limbs ;
None hear his low and hideous groan ;
  A silent shark swift by him swims.

Slowly the raft sinks down and rots ;
  The sun has faded now from view,
And in his lidless eyes are spots
  Of livid and atrocious blue.

TWO LOVES FOUND REFUGE.

A MOOD OF MADNESS.

Two loves found refuge in my happy heart,
One for my bride, one for the healing art;
Each of my spirit claimed an equal part.

No jealous phantom through the years could rise.
I drew new courage from her radiant eyes,
And grew in science and experience wise.

But, as my talent rose and waxed mature,
Love for my bride became more insecure,
Love for anatomy more deep and pure.

Until, oblivious of past cherished days,
Proud of strange studies and a city's praise,
My soul began to hate her winning ways.

Her kiss was odious! To her beauty blind,
I felt new longings, strange and undefined,
The fiend of science had perturbed my mind.

Each day a hellish wish, a mad desire
Throbbed in my veins with a demoniac fire.
Her smiling innocence aroused my ire.

She was a *subject* to my eyes alone ;
Not woman, forsooth, but so much flesh and bone,
Sinew, and blood, and skin, which were my own.

And I had lawful right, with foul intent,
I who for progress on this sphere was sent,
To use her body for experiment.

So in her wine I dropped consuming blight,
One moaning, shadow-haunted winter night,
And, watching, clutched my scalpel's handle tight.

Then, ere her eyes, that agony expressed,
Had closed forever, with impatient zest,
My hands were red dissecting her white breast.

1877.

INFLUENCE.

Oft when some weary city calmly sleeps,
   Oblivious for an hour of hate and spite,
   The livid moon, with sad, phantasmal light,
Strange vigils in the spotless azure keeps.

In ghostly ways she indolently creeps
   Among the sable glories of the night,
   And with insidious rays of deadly white
The dreamy town in one pale glamour steeps.

Then, should some mortal with enamored eye
   Gaze on her beauteous presence, chaste and proud,
     With maddening joy her luminous fibers beat,
And beams more potent from her brightness fly ;
   While men can hear the echo long and loud
     Of maniac laughter in a startled street !

April 19, 1878.

A WHIM.

If I were *sure* that kind and fecund Death
  Brought sweet annihilation and repose;
That with the sudden parting of our breath
  We ended for eternity our woes;

Yea, if I knew that I would ne'er arise
  In other forms, in other spheres remote,
I would applaud a God so great and wise
  And, with a prayer of rapture, cut my throat!

TEMPERAMENT

A cruel despot reigned ; each living thing
　　Shuddered before him ; in his vast domains
　　Hundreds of suffering wretches died in chains ;
The land was weary of their clamoring.

He loved to see wild hands in anguish cling ;
　　His heart was shut to pity and to pains,
　　While death made riot in his city's lanes,
Reigning with him, a dreaded, mightier king.

Then came upon the land a blighting blow ;
　　All that had blossomed on the fields was swept
　　　Skyward by tempests in their outraged power ;
For dreary months no shrub was known to grow,
　　And it was told that this harsh tyrant wept
　　　When pressing to his lips one withered flower,!

1878.

BEATA.

She walks among us in her innocence,
   Supreme in the blond glory of her hair,
   Serenely chaste, a vision of peace and prayer,
With dreamy Vestal eyes of blue intense.

None who have seen her purest glance know whence
   Comes its Madonna radiance soft and rare,
   When, pitying angel, she goes forth to share
With foul and leprous poor her opulence.

Men deem her candor from all evil free,
   And that her heart, in which no vice can grow,
   Is like her face, impeccable, divine.
But, ah ! the foolish world knows not how she,
   Flower-wreathed and passionate, in a bagnio,
     Has madly pressed lascivious lips to mine !

1877.

TO A FIRE-FLY.

Sprinkling with fire the midnight's utter dark,
    When the summer thickens mid the drowsy bowers,
Art thou ordained by God, oh, living spark,
    To guard the mystic passions of the flowers?

Or, with an ardent longing of delight,
    Dost thou for some sweet tryst of lilies burn?
Or art thou in the solitude of night
    The star for which the rose and violet yearn?

Perhaps thou art one of the Fury's tears,
    Dropped from a doomed and direful planet far,
Or yet, borne from the crash of dying spheres,
    Some luminous atom of a fallen star.

Perchance from altars where the grim Parsees
    Worshiped Ahura with melodious lyres,
Long centuries gone, thou comest over leas,
    A glittering remnant of their holy fires.

But no! For this thy glamour is not faint,
The chill of ages would its heat dispel ;
Such vividness, that burns without restraint,
Must be some floating particle of hell.

But why should I thy beauty thus compare,
Oh, most fantastic of ethereal things ?
For, when thy sheen illumes the soft June air,
Thou art more like a topaz tipped with wings.

Yet thou art fairest when Brazilian dames
Twine thee in bracelets on their white arms bare,
Or when they place the splendor of thy flames
Deep in the dusky torrents of their hair !

OBLIVION.

Far in far Colorado's cañoned gloom,
  Girt by the shadow of Titanic trees,
  Swept by the swift and eagle-haunted breeze,
There stands a desolate and forgotten tomb.

No hunter knows the dead one's name or doom;
  No soul to garland it has passed the seas;
  It lies there one of earth's sad mysteries,
Where cougars crawl, where weeds and nettle bloom.

The bounding bisons trample on the stone,
  The tempests lull the unknown form to rest.
  Unconsecrated, friendless and unblest,
It stands until the end of time, alone.
    Such is the oblivion that I fain would win
    When death relieves me of this life of sin.

1880.

A WISH.

It would be sweet to leave the joys of earth,
   And all the crowded ways that men invade,
   To seek the depths of some mysterious glade,
Untrodden since the universe had birth ;

To hear the wild birds fill with twittering mirth
   The solemn elms, and in the twilight shade
   Muse on the power supreme that all things made,
And with conflicting thoughts dispute His worth.

Yea, and to taunt this mighty Force unknown
   With skeptic scorning and a cynic sneer,
     Deeming his awful silence a disgrace ;
To doubt, and challenge Him upon His throne,
   In tones accusative to teach me fear,
     And then to suddenly meet Him, face to face !

1882.

FANTAISIE.

To please the insolence of my caprice,
  When Spleen has clutched me with its tireless hands,
My gentle Muse, white prophetess of peace,
Herald of utter and sublime release,
  In radiant peerlessness before me stands.
    While, mute, I watch with ravishment intense
    The avatars of her magnificence.

To chase the dolorous fancies from my brain,
  She rises as a Gaditana draped,
With languid eyes that hold the glow of Spain,
Silk-shod, mantilla-wrapped, now arch, now vain,
  Lissom and laughterful, and leopard-shaped !
    Warbling a *jota*, twirling cigarettes,
    Amid the clicking of mad castanets.

Then, should I frown, before me, svelte of air,
  Will glide in slow, voluptuous morbidesse,
The lithe, dusk beauty of a bayadere,
With gem-crushed ankles and dark sequined hair,

A pearl of Punjab in nude loveliness,
 Dancing in drowsy cadence, warm with flowers
 Beneath the palmy shade of Agra's towers.

Spinning huge tufts of flax in dreamy way,
 Again I see a Gretchen, rosy and blonde,
  In some quaint dorf upon the close of day,
  Listlessly humming an old roundelay,
 Or tender scraps of Heine, while beyond
  The rising moon o'er Ehrenbreitenstein
  Silvers the sleepy ripple of the Rhine!

Untempted still, the rapturous phantom dies,
 And, gravely fair and tearful, near me stands
A sweet Madonna, with consoling eyes
And heaven-illumined brows, who hears the sighs
 Of sinners kneeling with imploring hand,
  While all around me the transfigured air
  Seems purer by the mystery of prayer!

But I am desolate; and then appears
 A rough and painted siren, lewd and bold;
 A revel of flesh by vice bereft of tears,
Tempting my eager sense with lecherous leers,

Mad by the warmth of wine, the clink of gold,
  Whose shameless soul, polluted by sin's fire,
  Hoards nameless lusts ! Infernos of desire !

Again she comes as Artemis divine,
  Bathed in Greek moons, with lilies in her hair,
With eyes that dream of Ephesus, and shine
Below white brows of chastity, and pine
  Endymion's glance from slumber to ensnare ;
    Softly she passes o'er vague Attic grounds,
    Serene amid the clamor of her hounds !

Then should I, motionless, no rapture show,
  Clasping a jeweled nargileh unsipped,
I see again her perfect beauty glow,
The petted lily of the seraglio,
  With koholed lids and fingers henneh-tipped,
    Languidly chatting to her favorite birds
    In suave, voluptuous Circassian words.

Then should I murmur at such Orient grace,
  Mephitic odors from foul graves assault
My sense, and down dim vistas I can trace
The worm-gnawed outline of my Muse's face

Peering upon me from some putrid vault,
  To blight me by her pestilential breath,
  And cheer my *ennui* by the sight of Death!

And should I, shuddering, turn away in dread,
  From some wee window-sill, where mignonette
And heliotrope their balminess have spread,
I there can see the eager, bird-like head
  Of some blithe, merry, exquisite grisette,
    Feeding her pet canary in fond way,
    While singing you lewd songs by Béranger.

Alas! made callous by the blows of fate,
  No subtle metamorphosis of hers
Can ever hope by fancies to abate
The horror of a heart grown desolate,
  The cringing slave of spleen that nothing stirs;
    Grim spleen, oh, God! that dulls to me the immense
    Grand avatars of her magnificence!

1880.

CHIBOUQUE.

At Yeni-Djami, after Rhamadan,
  The Pacha in his palace lolls at ease ;
  Latakieh fumes his sensual palate please,
While round-limbed almées dance near his divan.

Slaves lure away *ennui* with flowers and fan ;
  And as his gem-tipped chibouque glows, he sees,
  In dreamy trance, those marvelous mysteries
The prophet sings of in the Al-Korán !

Pale, dusk-eyed girls, with sequin-studded hair,
  Dart through the opal clouds like agile deer,
    With sensuous curves his fancy to provoke ;
Delicious houris, ravishing and fair,
  Who to his vague and drowsy mind appear
    Like fragrant phantoms arabesqued in smoke !

FAMINE.

The father all haggard, the mother lean,
  In the bare room's solitude
Sat alone while the first-born slept serene—
  They had given it blood for food !

For weeks in the mart there had been no grain,
  And the sun had scorched the grass,
And in awful silence, in throes of pain,
  They counted the long hours pass.

For great heaps of gold they could buy no bread,
  God to prayer or curse was dumb,
And the streets were choked with their kindred dead,
  And they cried for death to come.

Then the haggard father, the mother lean,
  With a look of fierce delight,
Gazed long on the child that slept serene,
  And said, "We have food to-night."

March, 1878.

VILANELLE.

Spleen fills my soul with morbid pain ;
  I feel its chill touch o'er me creeping.
Ah ! when will Love return again ?

Before me shadowy phantoms wane,
  My livid lips in rank gall steeping ;
Spleen fills my soul with morbid pain !

Alas ! who can efface the stain
  Of desolation and of weeping ?
Ah ! when will love return again ?

To soothe or calm all prayer is vain ;
  For still, its eager vigil keeping,
Spleen fills my soul with morbid pain !

Of my hope-flowers that lack mild rain,
  An early harvest it is reaping.
Ah ! when will Love return again ?

I feel the fiends of blight and bane,
  Grim wings above my forehead sweeping.
Spleen fills my soul with morbid pain !

My passions, that so long have lain
  Forgotten, now are madly leaping.
Ah ! when will love return again ?

Ah ! grant me death, sweet God humane,
  For I am cursed awake or sleeping ;
Grim spleen has gorged my soul with pain,
  And love will ne'er return again !

WHIMS.

To please the morbid yearnings of my soul,
  And free myself from Spleen's atrocious bane,
I fain would mingle in complete control
  Churchly austerity with joys profane.

In lieu of dreary days that I despise,
  Although my hours upon the earth are brief,
I see as life flits by before mine eyes
  Great possibilities of supreme relief—

Relief that can bequeath a dual life,
  One that can soothe me as a loyal friend,
One that can blunt the sword of earthly strife,
  One that can bring indifference for an end.

It would be sweet to seek some desert spot,
  Some monkish cell or forest cavern bare,
Wherein to ponder on my hopeless lot
  And turn my rebel clamoring to prayer,

And then to leave it for the illumined town,
  Where jocund Carnival spawns mirth intense,
And, casting off the coarse and drugget gown,
  Revel in Sin's supremest insolence.

Ah ! sweet it were to riot in such way,
  Tho' marked unto the soul with *Ennui's* scar,
And blend in one, without a fool's dismay,
  The crucifix, the jest, the lupanar !

To see at morn the calm and flower-eyed nun
  Telling her beads in soft, ecstatic trance,
And court with smiles ere that same day be done
  A harlot's cold and scrutinizing glance.

Ay ! sweet unto the senses as a dream,
  'Twould be to humbly bow at vesper mass,
And at its end, in revelry supreme,
  To see the gold wine glitter in the glass !

But sweeter far to see the flawless moon
  Flooding La Trappe's monastic elms with sheen,
And leave it, in its blond celestial June
  Amid the clouds, for revelries unclean.

A humble crust at morn, at night the choice
  Of dainty viands and delicious fare ;
At morn an Ave told with vinous voice,
  At eve a ribald couplet debonair !

To tempt frail virtue to a hopeless snare,
  To steel the heart to every sacred vow ;
And to the solemn altar-steps repair
  With mirth or murder marked upon the brow.

Contrition ! Genuflections that allure !
  Calumny, lascivious fancies more than mad,
The Bible's lessons, marvelous and pure,
  And then the lecherous prowess of de Sade !

Oh, envied life ! to be the rampant beast
  Steeped in hot sin and from no vices free ;
To alternate the ruffian with the priest,
  The padre with the insolent grandee !

And feeling life hath nothing more than this
  No pleasure more delectable or sweet,
Until Death proves me with his icy kiss
  That heaven itself is but a grand deceit !

A MOOD OF HATRED.

I hate the red, intolerable sun
   That on my sorrowing brow pours searching light,
And wait in anger till its task be done.
       Delicious night !

But often, alas ! allured by treacherous sleep,
   In the dark midnight when the forest grieves,
I wake to see foul, luminous dawn-tints creep
       Between the leaves.

A flood of splendor in the happy skies
   Hails the calm, haughty sun, announcing day,
And blinds me, even before my dazzled eyes
       Can turn away!

It would be grand to live in those grim years
   As yet unborn, and feel, with soul aghast,
That God had doomed them here and in all spheres
       To be the last!

How sweet to enjoy the horror that each day,
  Slow, certain, fatal, to my mind could lend,
And see the world in terror and dismay
      Approach its end !

Then in sore anguish men in vain would cry
  And beg inexorable fate to spare ;
Piteous appeals would rend the hollow sky,
      Curses and prayer !

And I would witness with a mad delight
  Our mutual and inevitable doom,
Patiently waiting through the somber night
      And ghastly gloom,

That slowly o 'er the hopeless earth would fall,
  Never to rise ; to hear with eager dread
Strange, awful voices through dim spaces call,
      " *The sun is dead !* "

July 3, 1877.

THE HAREM.

Solemn Seraglio, stern sojourn,
What dormant passions in thee burn !
What ardors craving a return !

Splendor of splendors, gold and sheen,
Where priceless treasures damascene
Each lily-browed and languid queen.

Rivers of rubies, blent with pearls,
Trail in long scintillating whirls
O 'er swan-like necks and glossy curls.

Carpets of Smyrna, furry, deep,
Deaden the tread when eunuchs creep
Noiselessly where Sultanas sleep.

Hear the white foam from fountains fall,
Out through the marble-pillared hall,
Out where the dark gloom covers all.

Here repose houris, dreamlike fair ;
Eyes half amort by amorous care ;
Marvels of flesh, wonders of hair !

Khanouns arrayed in gemmy fire
Here chant upon the drowsy lyre,
Slowly, in honor of their sire.

Perfumes of attar scent the air,
Strange odors mingle everywhere,
Odors of love, odors of prayer.

Voluptuous music thrills through space,
In soft melodious throbs of grace,
Chasing the care from beauty's face.

Devoid of heart, of sense or soul,
Eunuchs stand watching, black as coal,
Stared at by peris from their Kóhol.

Scimitars crescent, dirks of gold,
Kandjars falcated, chill and cold,
Hang by their sides to guard the fold.

Pale Rouchen, saffron-tinged Asmé,
Nourmahal, Pembeh-al-Haré,
Leila the Rose, dusk Adilé,

Dream 'neath the shade of Abdul's crest ;
Dream in their beautiful unrest ;
Dream, fanning each irradiant breast.

Encrusted hookahs, amber-tipped,
Chibouques in gold and silver dipped,
By rich, red lips are slowly sipped,

While clouds of perfumed smoke arise
In dreamy opal to the skies,
Veiling the fire of lustrous eyes,

Veiling Sultanas, lithe and fair,
Mute with *ennui* and amorous care,
Marvels of flesh, wonders of hair !

A DREAM.

I dreamed that the great God, who rules us all,
   Was numbered with the nameless hosts of dead,
That He had perished beyond Time's recall,
   And all my soul was filled with speechless dread.

A holy horror o'er my senses crept,
   My mind groped wildly through the feverish dream ;
And then I thought, while painfully I slept,
   How can Death harm the Godhead all supreme ?

Then, in the awful silence of the night,
   A *something* swiftly in my presence came,
A mist, a phantom of seraphic light,
   A shape of fire, a vagrant film of flame !

A vision which no wretched mortal eyes
   Had ever seen upon this stricken sod,
And as I gazed a strange voice cried : "*Arise !*
   Worship me still ; I am the ghost of God !"

OVERGROWTH.

God spoke to haggard Death : " I bid thee cease
  Thy grim destruction of unnumbered years,
  For I am weary of my creatures' tears ;
Until I call thee, go thy way in peace."

And haughty Death, though scorning such release,
  Obeyed ; while millions on the ample spheres
  Marveled to see, with many doubts and fears,
Humanity in wondrous ways increase.

Until, grown sure of life, all men disdained
  The Mighty's boon and dreamed, in impious pride,
    That they with immortality were blessed.
Then God in wrath called Death with power regained,
  And suddenly the vile earth, terrified,
    Shrieked in the awful agonies of Pest !

TO AL-LEILA.

TURQUERIE.

Oh ! warm with the fire of thy perfumed caresses
    The chilly *ennui* of my desolate soul,
And rouse, by the swaying of undulate tresses,
    Love's sweetest excesses, with pleasure for goal.

Oh! touch with thy finger-tips, rosy with *henné*,
    Serenely the chords of my dreamy desire ;
As sweet as the words of one Prophet-God, when he
    Spake loud in Mosques many his precepts of fire.

Oh ! let thy dusk eyes lull with luminous flashes
    As light as a dream all my spirit's dismay ;
And sweep from my cheek, with thy tremulous lashes
    The tear-drop that dashes, or kiss it away.

Oh ! let me ne'er dream of a turbulent morrow ;
  Let ballads Arcadian upon thy lips ring,
And let me from rapture a calmer joy borrow,
  Sweet queller of sorrow, oh, more to me bring !

For, wearied and worn of the battle's red thunder,
  With yataghan broken, I fain now would rest,
All trusting in Allah, and craving sweet plunder
  Upon that white wonder, thy passionate breast !

A FANCY.

I feel the advent of the fatal hour,
  Bringing with it oblivion, and sigh ;
For, all unransomed from Death's evil power,
  I must prepare with fortitude to die.

And then I envy the eternal God,
  Who lent the universes shape and breath,
He who can rule the planets by a nod,
  He who knows not the agony of death.

METEMPSYCHOSIS.

My soul, by nature's law in ages past,
   Blended with color, perfume light and sound,
Before in ignominious rest, at last
   The unworthy heaven of my flesh was found.

When Eden, dreaming in delicious calm,
   Lulled the yet sinless Eve to chaste repose,
That soul brought to her sense ecstatic balm,
   Deep in the crimson petals of a rose.

By wondrous change it formed a deadly part
   Of the malarious wind by God's behest,
Ordained to awe grim Pharaoh's callous heart,
   And sweep fair Egypt with its blighting pest.

In Syrian groves it found a new release,
   In gentle twilights wooing drowsy flowers,
And, as a ray of the soft stars of Greece,
   It silvered with its sheen great Ilium's towers.

Long centuries fled ; transformed by powers unseen,
  Earthward it fell, a pearl unique and rare,
And on loud, ferial nights in splendor shone
  On Cleopatra's dusk and flowerful hair.

That soul, oh, horror! on one desolate morn,
  Innocent then as it is guilty now,
Formed of an awful crown the sharpest thorn
  That plunged a barb in Christ's forgiving brow.

*   *   *   *   *

On Isabeau de Barière's slender wrist
  It perched, a falcon, eager for its prey ;
And, as a dove, it guided to their tryst
  Dante and Beatrix, in the redolent May.

Through years of night, as the pale, feeble spark
  Of a poor fire-fly, it would humbly glow,
Till, resurrect, it thrilled the new-born lark
  That sang of dawn to amorous Romeo !

Cursed for this kind and timely warning rash,
  It crawled, a loathsome python, sleek and black,
Until the day when it became the flash
  That gleamed upon the dirk of Ravaillac !

For lordlier uses, its strange essence came
  Through centuries to be a scrap of sun,
And over Wagram's desolating flame
  Prompted the genius of Napoleon.

A formless atom then, it sped along
  Thro' unknown spheres of which it held no part,
Till, as a sweet inspired, melodious song,
  It softly stirred in Donizetti's heart.

Oh, soul serene! Oh, soul supremely fair!
  Thou, that like winds wast vigorous and fresh,
What devil doomed thy peerlessness to share
  The pain and passion of *my* hateful flesh?

THE MUSKETEERS.

D'ARTAGNAN.

Thou art eternal, tho' the mighty brain
   That brought thee forth from shadowland is dead ;
   In thee he lives imperishable, wed
To every joy of thine, to every pain.

Thy valiant deeds indelible remain ;
   We love thy young, hot blood in battle shed,
   And by thy every daring deed are led
More firmly admiration to retain.

Whene'er thy name defiant meets mine eyes,
   I see thee hurrying on a foaming steed
     With valorous Porthos ripe from war's alarms.
And then again in sadness I surmise
   How thy fond spirit must have bled, indeed,
     When pressing thy dead Constance in thine arms !

ARAMIS.

Thy heart was one of craft, yet thou wast brave
  As steel Castilian ; but ambition's bane
  Lurked in the subtle essence of thy brain,
And naught beyond this passion did 'st thou crave.

Battling for decades by an open grave,
  Thou did 'st not swerve, nor did 'st thou e'er restrain
  Thy mental greeds, thy ceaseless chase for gain,
Which at the end thy comrade could not save.

Ah ! nobler far wast thou on that blue morn,
  When Porthos, sinking in a grave of stone,
    Fell like a Hercules, no more to rise.
Then, anguished, mute, irresolute, forlorn,
  Thy heart lay broken by his dying groan,
    And tears surprised the desert of thine eyes.

PORTHOS.

Oh, child-like giant ! in thy massive frame
  A heart that grasped the world did nobly beat.
  Type of the gallant musketeer complete,
Thy blow was death, thy rapier was a flame !

Pleased with a bauble, a baronnie name,
    No fertile plain or castle-crowned retreat
    Could stay the riotous rushing of thy feet,
When time for wonderful adventure came !

I see thee battling with a hero's zeal,
    Brave in that blessed land where all are brave,
    Eager for *estocade* at dawn or gloom ;
And then, again, on pinnacled Belle Isle,
    I see the grim, red hell-light of thy cave,
        And watch thee die in thy Titanic tomb !

ATHOS.

Thy mind was fit for prehistoric time,
    When man was perfect, ere the birth of guile ;
    I love the gentle glamour of thy smile ;
I love thy heart beyond all taint or crime.

No passion base e'er touched thee with its slime ;
    In thee dwelt radiant honor and no wile ;
    And not a thought ignoble could defile
Thy soul, that ever higher seemed to climb !

Whene'er of all thy prowesses I read,
  I see thee, grave, before me, with thy wine,
    The mellow *vin d' Anjou* thou lov'dst so well ;
And then again, Homeric, on thy steed,
  Clearing the foemen with a smile divine,
    Below the embattled walls of La Rochelle !

ENIGMA.

My bosom bounds with rapturous faith elate ;
  Youth in its spring stirs gently thro' my veins ;
  Consciously strong, I fear no future pains ;
My sinless soul as yet knows naught of hate.

Unyielding, I can bear life's onerous weight,
  Scorning the anger it for me retains ;
  But, ah ! I dread the woman whom Fate ordains
To make me vile among all men, or great.

The awful query ever thrills my lips :
  Shall the rich virgin treasuers of my heart
    Be given to some chaste creature, lily-frail ;
Or shall my soul, plunged down in dark eclipse,
  Be lured to ruin by the infernal art
    Of some white Eve-like harlot, passion-pale ?

1867.

IMPLACABLE.

Upon the desert of my sorrowing mind
    I nursed a little, unpretending flower,
Hoping within its virgin core to find
    A sweet perfume in tribulation's hour.

'Twas all I loved, 'twas all that made me glad,
    This cherished bud I guarded as my breath ;
And when God knew the great love that I had,
    He struck the harmless blossom unto death !

WHEN THE SNOW FALLS.

The spider Spleen, that slowly and subtly weaves
   Its odious web upon my golden thought,
   Left no foul hint forgotten or unsought
To taint a swerving soul that doubts and grieves.

My faith, once strong, is now like withered leaves
   In the chill vortex of a tempest caught,
   And, by the artful world's vile lessons taught,
I know that smiling chastity deceives.

There is no purity on earth, I cried ;
   Gold of a virgin can a plaything make ;
     There lives no stainless thing save burning fire !
While the pure snow upon the lowlands wide,
   God's silent answer, fluttered as I spake,
     But nothing proved ; the sun will make it mire.

1878.

LIKE POOR OPHELIA.

Like poor Ophelia, pale, Murillo-fair,
   The beauteous one, whose love once fired my brain,
   Roams thro' my dwelling, silent and insane,
In the blond splendor of her tangled hair,

Unconsciously she bares the round and rare
   Carrara of her breast without a stain,
   While I, who of her beauty am still vain,
Smile grimly at her dull and vacant stare.

When, like an amorous cat, she toward me bounds,
   I love to see her, warm with wanton fire,
     Invent endearments new in bizarre wise ;
And when she lisps odd, idiotic sounds,
   To watch the inferno of her strange desire
     Gleam weirdly in her colorless dull eyes !

Nov. 26, 1877.

DREAM OF DEATH.

A MOOD OF MADNESS.

Pondering upon my many woes, I lay
  One sad night in my hope-deserted room ;
Even sleep my febrile call would not obey,
And, with rebellious thoughts, awaiting day,
I calmly watched the blood-red coals decay,
  Sprinkling with lurid gleams the uncertain gloom.

The ominous silence was akin to pain ;
  My uneven pulses only gently stirred ;
Oppressed by the strange stillness, I was fain
With incoherent clamoring to gain
Release from such unhealthy and morbid strain,
  And strove to rise ; but suddenly I heard

A low, soft voice that called me by my name
  In such sweet tones, that, turning in my bed,
I scanned the room, to see from whence it came.

It seemed so strange, for my vile heart could claim
No friend or love ; then suddenly a flame
   Hissed fiercely from the hearth ; the coals were dead !

Then, in the utter darkness, a something passed
   Before me as I listened, mute and thrilled.
It seemed as if an icy cavern vast
Had opened, and, with blighting fury, cast
The chill and piercing air in gusts aghast.
   Awe, I ne'er felt for God, my spirit filled.

And then again the same voice came to me,
   Like some sweet song sung by a freezing breath,
And cried, "Oh, man ! if thou can 'st fearless be ;
If, like thy soul, thy flesh from dread is free,
Hark to my words and listen to my plea :
   Know that I love thee, *and my name is Death.*

" I love thee for thy hatred of mankind,
   And the imprisoned lusts that chafe within
Thy brain, to purity and conscience blind.
I love thee for the rancor of thy mind,
That ever new and odious crime can find ;
   I love thee for thy infamy and sin.

"Thy soul, by fates unpitying aged and galled,
  Prayed to no thorn-crowned God in its despair.
By thoughts of my omnipotence unappalled,
Thou liv'st in unbelief, by spleen enthralled ;
Earth hath no rose wherein thou hast not crawled,
  Oh, mortal worm I madly love, and spare !

"If, then, I awe thee not, and thou art bold,
  I will take human shape and, love-possessed,
Offer thee joys undreamt of and untold.
Shrink not, nor tremble, dreaming Death is cold,
But, like warm adders, let thine arms enfold
  These icy charms no mortal has caressed."

"Oh, Death ! *White, warm, voluptuous Death !*" I cried,
  "Take the frail soul that God and world defies !
Take all, my blood, my hate, my flesh, my pride !"
And, as I spake, I felt a vague form glide,
  And saw, with thrills of rapture and surprise,
  A strange, weird woman with delicious eyes.

  *   *   *   *   *   *

All ye who live when I am dead, have care
  Of that strange being from dreadful travail torn,
From one who knows no mercy, heeds no prayer ;

Fear more than God, ever and everywhere,
The monster who, in moments of despair,
From my grand hate and Mother Death was born !

Feb. 23, 1878.

THE SPIRIT OF RUINS.

I have hung my misty ivy over all
   The pomps of antique Rome, and the gray blight
   Of my grim touch upon the Rhine doth smite
Full many a haughty burg and crumbling wall.

In ways severe, implacable, I fall
   Where colonnaded Parthenons rise white
   Into the nimbus of the soft Greek light,
Or where proud Baalbec's dismal shades appall.

Oh, morbid joy have I, when towns of towers,
   And insolent Karnacs, by grave sphinxes girt,
Perish before my dark, destructive powers.
   And I am glad to view, with eyes alert,
The mute magnificence of their leafless bowers,
   Their glory shattered in palatial dirt !

TYLL OWLGLASS.

OBIIT 1530.

Like some mad meteor plunging through the dark
   Abysmal vastness of the silent night,
   Leaving a smoky trail of scintillant light
Behind, its weird and luminous route to mark,

So did'st thou thro' the Middle Ages cark ;
   And thy rare humor and thy jesting bright
   Dispelled the gloom of men, who, awed by fright,
Prayed for the dawn of which *thou wast the lark !*

From that grim, tyrant-haunted, monkish time
   Of superstition, bigotry and ill,
     No kindlier record would have reached our ears
Than one long, dolorous tale of blood and crime,
   Had it not been for thee !　And we hear still
     Thy mellow laughter ebbing through the years !

Dec. 5, 1877.

BITTER TEARS.

RONDEAU.

O, bitter tears unchecked, that rise again,
What balm to my dead heart can ye bestow?
How can your dreary advent e 'er contain
Mandragoras for my supremest woe?

A faded flower heeds not the gentle rain,
That to revive its loveliness were fain ;
And while sad memory's smoldering embers glow
Ye can not blot the dark past from my brain,
          O, bitter tears !

That flood, my will is powerless to restrain,
Adds to pale grief a keener, deeper trace ;
Morbid self-pity I would fain forego ;
So leave me to the majesty of pain,
To suffer and be silent ; cease to flow,
          O, bitter tears !

A MOOD OF MADNESS.

TO —

I asked the pallid woman I called wife,
  Chaste, nun-like being, whose will I can not break,
To leave for sin and lust her prayerful life,
  And pledge with me a toast for hell's sweet sake.

I longed to chafe her calm soul with alarms,
  And, with Satanic craft, its candor taint ;
Wrench it forever from all churchly charms,
  And give the demon access to the saint.

This bigot-gnat that worries God all day,
  Filling his temples with loud psalms and sighs,
Grew pale and answered, " No," as in dismay
  She gazed upon me with her Christ-like eyes.

Ah ! from that moment a resistless fate
  Dropped in my fungous heart of gall and gloom
Innumerable seeds of rankest hate,
  To germ and in vile vegetations bloom.

She would not pledge with me, but spurned me there,
　　As angels would a spitting toad malign ;
She left me for some unctuous orgy of prayer—
　　The fool, the triple fool—alone with wine !

　　　*　　　　*　　　　*　　　　*　　　　*

Oh, luminous hell ! thy gall to me is sweet,
　　From thee my sick, sad spirit never shrank ;
Remember how in vassalage complete,
　　While she belched litanies, to thee I drank.

Did God she sued, grown weary of her voice,
　　Protect her from the inferno in me rife ?
Did not her hymn-deaf cherubim rejoice
　　When at her throat they saw my gleaming knife ?

She prayed too much ; that night her severed head
　　'Mid fruits and viands on my table stood !
Sweet saint ! for her an aureole of red
　　I made with long wet hair and clotted blood !

And then I closed her Christ-like eyes divine,
　　That cursed me ; and her great dead thirst to slake,
I filled her livid mouth with glorious wine,
　　And the night long she drank for hell's sweet sake !

July 27, 1878.

IN THE FOREST OF FONTAINEBLEAU.

Deep in the tangled mazes of a wood,
    The shady haunt of many roaming herds,
In summers' idleness I musing stood,
    Charmed by the soft *staccati* of the birds.

The giant oaks that towered in stately might
    Seemed born the soul of winter to defy ;
Huge, rugged Samsons among trees, whose height
    And spreading boughs colossal pierced the sky.

And then I wondered, what will be the fate
    Of all the green magnificence spread here ?
Will flame its swaying glory violate,
    Or will the storms of centuries leave it sere ?

Who knows ? The lordly tree that yonder stands,
    Proud of the robin that upon it sings,
Felled to the earth by rough and callous hands,
    May be the prop of palaces for kings !

Its mate stupendous, brooding there apart,
  Dismembered and uncrowned before all eyes,
May yet be changed into a whirring dart,
  To kill yon eagle soaring thro' the skies !

Another, refuge of the hunted stag,
  That seeks its shadow with a panting breath,
May yet uphold the proud, triumphant flag
  That France unfurls for liberty or death !

A hideous shape, before a brawling throng,
  Yon old and knotted trunk may yet be seen,
Bereft of leaves and of the linnet's song,
  Turned to the horror of a guillotine !

And, ah ! perchance that other standing there
  In leafy splendor, shading now my head,
May be the coffin, still unformed and bare,
  Destined to hold and keep me with the dead !

1881.